THE Psychic EDGE

Patrick Devaney

MENTOR

This Edition first published 2000 by

MENTOR BOOKS
43 Furze Road,
Sandyford Industrial Estate,
Dublin 18.

Tel. (01) 295 2112/3   Fax. (01) 295 2114
e-mail: admin@mentorbooks.ie
www.mentorbooks.ie

ISBN: 1-84210-020-3

Cover Illustration: Jimmy Lawlor
Typesetting, editing, design and layout by
MENTOR BOOKS

Printed in Ireland by ColourBooks

CONTENTS

Patrick Devaney was born in Croghan, Co. Roscommon. His published work includes two novels for teenagers, *Rua the Red Grouse* and *The Stranger and the Pooka*, and a collection of poems, *Searching for Updraughts*. He lives in Maynooth and teaches in the local Post-Primary School.

ACKNOWLEDGEMENTS

My thanks are due to my wife, Cheryl, who not only offered incisive criticism but also typed and corrected a major portion of the manuscript; to my children, Clare, Catherine, Deirdre and in particular, Aileen and Conor, who gave illuminating insights into the culture and language of teenagers; to my sister Christina for information on Boyne salmon and scrutinising the various drafts; to Robert Leak for an up-to-date map of New York City; to Catherine Heslin for typing the first five chapters; to Sean Ashe for placing the computers in Maynooth Post-Primary School at my disposal; to Sheila Downey and Marcella Carroll for helpful suggestions about typing; to Janette Meehan for efficiently typing five chapters; to Dermot Nangle for copying floppy disks and getting the typescript ready for publication and to Oifig an tSoláthair, Baile Átha Cliath, for the quotation from *An Fhiannuidheacht*.

For

Mary, Cathal, Emily and Christina

'D'ith an giolla an bradán leis sin. Agus is é
sin tráth do tugadh an déad feasa d'Fhionn,
an uair do chuir sé a órdóg 'na bhéal.'
'With that the youth ate the salmon. And that
is the occasion that the tooth of knowledge
was given to Fionn, the time he put his
thumb in his mouth.'

Cormac Ó Cadhlaigh
An Fhiannuidheacht

'The Rulers of the Killing Ground are
coming out to play
Everyone thinking: who they going to play
with today?'

Adrian Mitchell
'Back in the Playground Blues'

PROLOGUE

The unexpected tug on the line set David's heart leaping. 'I've got a big bite!' he shouted, holding frantically on to the hazel pole with both hands.

'Keep a steady pull!' Uncle Fintan advised as he laid his rod on the bank and hurried over. 'That's it, David! Good boy!'

'I can't hold him any longer.' David felt the reel turning in his hand as the great fish struggled to escape. 'You take it.'

'No.' His uncle remained calm. 'Just let the line out slowly. Give him a chance to run. That's it. Steady now.'

'He's getting away,' David cried.

'No, he's not.' Uncle Fintan tilted the hazel pole with the palm of his hand. 'He's just making for that pool upstream. We'll let him run a bit. Dammit! To think he passed up my mallard wing for a worm. Isn't that— Watch out! Keep him away from the rocks! If he snags the line, he'll break it. Crikey!'

With a sudden lurch, the great fish broke through the surface, turned over with a flash of gleaming silver scales and plunged underwater again.

'It's him!' Uncle Fintan cried. 'It's the same fellow I've been after. David, you've hooked the King of the Boyne!'

David barely heard. He was wading into the river, ignoring his wet jeans and the mud sucking at his sneakers. This was his chance to prove that he wasn't a geek. Wouldn't Aisling be impressed if she could see him now? Oops! His foot slid into a depression, throwing him off balance. Without letting go of the pole he managed to right himself, though the water was lapping his thighs.

Uncle Fintan plunged into the river and grabbed David's shoulders, steadying the boy. 'Reel in your slack!' he shouted. 'That's it. Keep a steady pull. No, not too much!'

Slowly they backed out of the water, David bracing the pole against his abdomen with his left hand while he turned the reel with his right. Once or twice he stumbled but with his uncle's help he eventually climbed back on to the bank.

The salmon raced across the river, cleaving the surface as the line tightened.

'He's tiring!' Uncle Fintan chortled. 'Just play him like that, nice and easy. Oh boy, what a beauty! Look at the curl of his lower jaw and the wicked gleam in his eye! Wait now while I get my net.'

Three minutes later, Uncle Fintan deftly moved the hoop of the net under the giant fish then with a smooth upward sweep lifted him out of the water. David winced as his uncle hit the writhing salmon across the back of the head with a rock before removing the hook.

'Here, David.' He presented the heavy, slippery prize to his nephew. 'You carry him. If only we had a camera.'

While his uncle gathered up the tackle, David tried to ignore the salmon's glazed eye and the blood oozing from the broken flesh. Already he was shivering as the raw February breeze cut through his wet jeans.

In a fever of impatience they trotted back to the house where his uncle set about gutting the salmon. After changing into dry clothes, David helped to prepare lunch; laying the table, slicing bread and even making tea, something his mother would never let him do for fear he might scald himself. While his uncle was changing in the bedroom, David watched the grill where two fragrant salmon steaks were cooking. He felt proud that he was the one who had provided this treat.

All this time his uncle kept up a constant flow of talk. 'I tell you it's no ordinary salmon,' he shouted from the bedroom. 'That fellow has returned from the ocean at least three years running. Just imagine the kind of intelligence that takes: swimming thousands of miles across the Atlantic then down through the North Channel into the Irish Sea and somehow he finds his way back into the Boyne, the very river he started out from. And once in the river he evades every attempt by all the poachers and fishermen between here and Drogheda to nab him: net, trap, spinner, fly, worm, shrimp – you name it.'

'But he took my worms,' David pointed out.

'That's just it.' His uncle entered the kitchen in his socks, tightening his belt. 'He wanted you to catch him. If you hadn't come for your mid-term break, he'd still be out there in the river, thumbing his nose at me.'

The idea of a salmon thumbing his nose at anybody struck David as ridiculous. Still, it was nothing to some of the daft notions his uncle had, such as his belief that salmon were once people whose spirits had entered the water when they died and that the one they had caught, the

King of the Boyne, had been reborn again and again. Maybe living alone on a small farm had left him a bit batty. Not that David disliked him: Uncle Fintan was generosity itself and he did know a lot about nature.

'Here,' his uncle removed a piece of the cooking salmon with a fork, 'you taste it.'

'No,' David protested. 'Without you I'd never have landed him. You have the first bite.'

'Nonsense.' His uncle moved the fork closer. 'You're poor Michael's son, Lord have mercy on him. What would an old fogey like me need with second sight?'

Gingerly David took the steaming morsel between his thumb and forefinger and popped it into his mouth, licking his fingers to cool them. Immediately an image of his mother toppling off a stool in the guest bedroom flashed into his mind.

'Well?' His uncle looked at him expectantly. 'What happened?'

'It's nice.' David thought it best not to mention what he had seen. After all, it might just have been his imagination.

'Oh.' His uncle's face fell. 'I thought you might have been given the same power that young Fionn MacCumhail got when he tasted the Salmon of Knowledge. Maybe if you chewed your thumb the way he did . . . '

Feeling stupid, David went through the motions of chewing his right thumb.

'Yes, that's it.' Uncle Fintan's face glowed with expectation. 'Now what do you see?'

'Nothing,' David assured him.

'In that case we might as well tuck in.' Uncle Fintan forked the steaks off the grill on to two plates. 'You're certain you didn't have . . . an inner sighting, a vision?'

David shook his head. The combination of buttered soda cake and hot salmon was delicious. 'Uncle,' he spoke with his mouth full, 'why can't I live here with you?'

'Wouldn't you miss Darren and Emma?' His uncle tried to hide his pleasure.

'Those two?' David frowned as he recalled his younger brother and sister.

'And what about your mother?' His uncle buttered another slice of bread. 'How would she manage without you?'

'She'd have Doug.' David laid down his knife and fork.

'Now, David,' Uncle Fintan spoke gently, 'you mustn't be hard on your mother. She's trying to do her best by all of you. And Michael, Lord have mercy on him, didn't leave her with much.'

David said nothing. He knew that his father had had a drinking problem but that didn't make it right for his mother to take up with a truck driver just a few years after his death.

'Come now.' His uncle touched his hand. 'I'm really flattered, David, that you want to stay with me but, apart from anything else, the school here isn't a patch on the one in Lisheen. And you have your friends there.'

'No, I don't.' David kept his eyes on his half-eaten meal. 'I hate the Post Primary.'

'Whisht!' His uncle sounded uncomfortable. 'Sure we all thought we hated school. But when you're—'

The phone interrupted him.

'That was Doctor O'Brien's receptionist,' he said when he returned from the hall. 'I'll have to drive you home, David. Your mother has just sprained her ankle.'

CHAPTER 1

It was a dull Tuesday morning. David pushed up the bottom of his school bag to ease the pain caused by the straps biting into his shoulders. His mother had kept him home the previous day to do the housework while she rested her sprained ankle. Today she had shunted him off to school because Doug was arriving back from Holland. David wished he didn't have to go.

He was walking on his own as usual. On the opposite footpath a crowd of boys and girls in navy blue uniforms – which had given rise to their nickname, 'the Bluebottles' – straggled along, chatting and laughing. Now and then somebody glanced in his direction, then turned away before he could smile. He wished Jonathan, who had been his best friend in National School, was with him but his parents had sent him as a boarder to Hollybrook College in Kilbride. The only bright spot on the horizon was the certainty that he would be near Aisling Murphy at least once or twice today, though she probably wouldn't spare him a second glance. On the other hand, there would be the usual three gorillas who certainly would.

As he approached the entrance to Pine Lawns Estate, a sturdy Black boy with close-cropped hair, wearing the school trousers and sweater, came ambling out. David remembered having seen him near the chip shop before the mid-term break.

'Hi, man.' He gave David a big smile.

'Hi.' David decided to be friendly.

'My name's Billy.' The Black boy spoke with an American accent. 'Billy Jones. What's yours?'

David told him and asked his age.

'Fifteen,' Billy said. 'My mother's working for Compu-Tel. We're only going to be in Ireland for a year or so. Mom says I have to attend your school or return to the States. So what's it like?'

'Lisheen Post Primary? Okay, I suppose.' David didn't want to admit it was bad. 'The teachers don't hassle you if you keep your head down.'

'Man, if they hassle me, I'll tell them where to get off,' Billy vowed with good humoured self-confidence. 'In our High School in Queens—'

He was interrupted by a shout.

'Hey, Byrne, who's your darkie friend?' John Cox, who was known as Johnno, yelled across the road.

'What you saying, man?' Billy demanded. 'Got a potato stuck in your throat?'

'Go back to the jungle, Coco Pops,' Johnno taunted.

'Just ignore him.' David chewed nervously on his thumb.

Suddenly an image of a truck bearing down on Cox flashed into his mind. He saw Johnno falling in front of the huge wheels.

'I won't take garbage like that from any jerk,' Billy

growled. 'You're a big man with a big mouth,' he shouted at Johnno. 'But that's only because you have your buddies with you. Come over here on your own, man, and we'll see how much guts you got.'

'Righto.' Ignoring the heavy morning traffic Johnno made to cross the road, right in the path of an articulated lorry. There was a squeal of brakes as the massive vehicle skidded to a halt inches from Johnno, who promptly sank to the ground.

'What the hell do you think you're playing at?' the driver screamed out of the window. For a fleeting moment David thought it was Doug then he realised it wasn't a Lisheen Transport truck. 'If I come out to you I'll kick your butt from here to Dublin,' the driver threatened. He opened the door of the cab just as Johnno sprang up and retreated to the safety of the footpath.

'Bloody halfwit!' the driver fumed while with a loud grating he put the engine back in gear.

'Why can't you watch where you're going, dad?' Johnno jeered as the lorry moved off.

'Cool!' Billy exclaimed. 'Is that dude in Senior High?'

'Hmm,' David mumbled.

His head was swimming. Had he actually foreseen what had happened or was his imagination playing tricks on him? He recalled the salmon struggling on the line and his Uncle Fintan exulting, 'That's him! That's the King of the Boyne!'

'Did you hear me?' Billy's voice broke in on his thoughts. 'Is he in Senior High?'

'Johnno?' David looked at the crowd of pupils gathered in admiration about their hero. 'No, he's in Third Year. He should be in Transition Year but he was kept back.'

'Then he must be an okay guy.' Billy sounded pleased.

'He's just a plonker.' David was fearful that Billy would soon desert him for his enemy. 'You heard what he called you. That's his style.'

In the Main Hall Billy had to wait for his appointment with Diggy, Mr Duignan the vice principal. Eyes downcast, David made his way up the crowded corridor to Resource Area One, where the Second Years had their lockers. He wished he could be laid back like Billy but the thought of Johnno's bunch, and even some fellows such as Dermo Campbell from his own class, waiting for him at morning break filled him with dread.

His worst fears were confirmed when he found the door of his locker kicked in. Tension closed on his stomach like an iron clamp. His English and maths textbooks and his pocket calculator were gone but, worst of all, the Omega watch his father had given him was nowhere to be seen. He had hidden it in one corner before the last PE class and in the excitement of hurrying out of school that evening for the mid-term break had forgotten to retrieve it. Who could have taken such a personal thing?

Like a small child, tears welled in his eyes. He began to chew the inside of his thumb as a wave of nausea swept over him, and he was carried into swirling mist where his father's face loomed before him. The mist cleared and he saw Johnno and his sidekicks, Iggy MacDermott and Jim Mullooly, walking into a pawnshop with the name 'Barretts' in big letters over the front.

'Byrne!' The voice of Mr Keane, the principal, thundered in his ears. 'Why aren't you in your classroom?'

'Please, sir, my locker was kicked in,' David explained.

18

'All right. I'll get Mick to repair it.' His voice softened a little. 'In the meantime get into class for roll call.'

The first class was English. Tubby, the old bald-headed teacher, rambled on about Goldsmith's Village Schoolmaster, totally unaware that David had no textbook.

'A man severe he was, and stern to view,' Tubby intoned with relish. David's mind strayed to what he had experienced at the locker. Following on the vision he'd had of Johnno falling before the truck and the one of his mother spraining her ankle, it almost seemed as if he might have second sight. Could Uncle Fintan have been right about the salmon? No, that was just nonsense. How could you get knowledge from eating a fish? Still, it was an exciting thought. Suppose he chewed his thumb again to see what happened?

He put his thumb in his mouth but no vision came. Maybe it only worked at certain times? Nevertheless, he would go up to Dublin on Saturday. The only pawnshop he knew of was in Capel Street. If Johnno, Mack and Muller were going to flog his watch . . .

'I know, Master Byrne, that Goldsmith speaks of "the boding tremblers"',' Tubby's voice roused him, 'but I doubt the pupils ended up reverting to childhood behaviour.'

The class tittered as David, red faced, took his thumb out of his mouth.

'No, don't tell me,' Tubby went on, 'you forgot your textbook. All right then, you can look in with Master Campbell – but have it tomorrow.'

'Here, Davina,' Dermo hissed, shoving an open book towards the edge of the desk.

David sat as far from Campbell as he could without making it too obvious. Dermo's brother, Nick, was one of

the hard men in Fifth Year. He also had a sister in Leaving
Cert who wore a nose ring. Dermo's book was torn and he
had scribbled over the pages. David thought of his own
clean book and the Omega watch his father had given him;
it was made of gold. Would Johnno really try to pawn it?
Well, Saturday would tell.

CHAPTER 2

At morning break David found Billy chatting up a group of Class 2F girls.

'Have you really spoken to Michael Jackson?' Mary O'Connor, a skinny redhead, was asking.

'Sure,' Billy informed her. 'He's a brother.' The girls giggled at this answer.

'I met him in a nightclub on 125th Street,' Billy went on. 'That's in Harlem – I guess you've heard of Harlem? I'm also a friend of Tiger Woods – you know, the golfer?'

David was about to slink away but Billy called out, 'Hey, David, I want you to meet the girls in my class.'

The girls' faces fell as David sidled up, munching an apple to hide his nervousness.

'We saw Michael Jackson at a concert in the RDS,' Rebecca Dolan, a ponytailed brunette with freckles, announced. 'It was on last July.'

'Oh!' Billy looked surprised. 'I guess you guys know as much about him then as I do.'

'Well, if it isn't The Fresh Prince of Belair.' Johnno and his two sidekicks halted beside the group. Mack and

21

Muller were chewing bars and Johnno had a can of Pepsi.

'Hi, man.' Billy gave Johnno a white-toothed grin. 'That was a cool move with the truck. You should have seen this guy playing chicken with a forty-ton truck.' He turned to the girls. 'Dave here saw it too.'

'That's right,' David nodded. He could see that Johnno was thrown off balance by the compliment.

'You've a great gift of the gab,' Johnno growled.

'Yeah, man. I kissed the Blarney Stone,' Billy mocked.

'You're very sure of yourself for a blow-in.' Johnno measured him with his eye. 'Are you as good with your fists as you are with your mouth?'

'Look, man, I'm not into fighting.' Billy held out his hands, palms up.

'So you're yellow too,' Johnno sneered.

The girls drew back as if uncertain about what might occur but at that moment Diggy, the vice principal, who was standing near the sports trophy cabinet, approached.

'Looking for a little aggro?' he said to Cox.

'No, sir,' Johnno assured him. 'Just being friendly.'

'Yes,' Diggy observed drily, 'you're a very friendly bloke. Now you and your mates take yourselves out of here or you'll be picking up rubbish for the next half hour.'

'Don't mind those creeps,' Sinéad Foley, an athletic looking blonde with braces on her teeth, advised Billy when Diggy moved off.

'Who minds?' Billy shrugged. 'I guess they're just a few punks looking for a reputation.'

David didn't listen to the rest of the conversation. He had caught sight of Aisling strolling up with her friends. Her ash-blonde hair framed her delicate, oval face with its luminous grey eyes. She caught him staring at her and he reddened. What would he do if she joined the group around Billy? He dropped his gaze as she passed, then cursed himself for being such a dope. Maybe he could foresee how she would react the next time they met?

Casually he placed the side of his thumb in his mouth and gnawed it. Nothing happened, either because he was too agitated to concentrate or else because she was going to ignore him. Nevertheless, his mind was like a dark room into which sunlight had penetrated. What did it matter whether or not she spoke to him so long as he could look forward to being dazzled like that every time she passed? The sudden ringing of the bell put an end to his reflections. If he hurried he would get to class before the punks – as Billy had called Johnno and his sidekicks – returned.

During lunch time he joined the crowd who had gathered round the basketball court to watch a game between Second Years and Third Years. Normally, the Third Years would not have lowered themselves to play Second Years but Billy had issued a challenge which, the punks insisted, they couldn't ignore. Now Billy was delighting the spectators with his ability to weave and dribble, much to the chagrin of Johnno, who time and again failed to block him. When the game was almost at an end, Father Moore, the chaplain, who was acting as referee, penalised Johnno for fouling, giving Billy a free shot. Since the scores were even, this shot would decide the outcome. Billy took the ball, bounced it a few times, raised it chin high, then lobbed it neatly into the basket. The crowd went wild. Without waiting for the final whistle, the girls rushed onto the court to surround their champion. Only David detected the look of near hatred on Johnno's face.

That evening Mrs Jones picked Billy up. As he watched the red MG nosing its way through students pouring out the gate, David wondered how he would get home without being set upon. When he was walking by the ramp down to the canal the punks emerged from behind the roadside wall and surrounded him.

'Come for a little chat.' Johnno steered him down to the towpath and under the bridge, where there was a narrow passage bordering the water.

'What do you want?' David tried to keep the tremor out of his voice.

'We ask the questions.' Mack punched him in the stomach, so that he doubled over with pain.

'Now, Davina,' Johnno removed David's school bag, 'we want you to help us. Will you?'

David looked at the grinning faces of Mack and Muller, then straight into Johnno's narrowed eyes. 'Isn't it enough that you kicked in my locker and stole my books and watch?' he screamed.

'Wait! Hold it!' Johnno held up his hand to restrain Muller who was about to thump their victim. 'This is a serious accusation and it deserves to be dealt with. Who told you we took your stuff?' He twisted David's arm till he winced.

'Nobody told me,' he cried out. 'I was just guessing.'

'Well, you guessed wrong and for that you'll pay.' Johnno nodded to his sidekicks, who each grabbed David by an arm and leg and held him, head down, a few inches above the water.

'Duck him,' Johnno commanded.

David closed his eyes and mouth in terror as the cold water touched his scalp. But then he was suddenly jerked up.

Opening his eyes, he found the cut-stone wall almost touching his face.

'That's just a warning,' Johnno explained. 'Now say sorry.'

'Sorry,' David mumbled and he was lifted roughly and set on his feet. The water ran down his forehead, into his eyes and down the back of his neck.

'Now listen carefully,' Johnno instructed. 'You're to invite Coco Pops – what's his name? Billy? – You're to invite Billy Coco Pops for a walk along the canal Friday evening. We just want to have a chat with him, nothing more. We won't lay a hand on him. Honest.'

'And suppose he doesn't want to go?' David asked.

'Then you'll be going for a swim.' Johnno patted his face. 'Let him go, fellas. We'll be talking to you during the week,' he called out as David trudged up the ramp. 'Bye, Davina.'

'What delayed you and what on earth happened to your hair?' his mother demanded when David arrived home.

'We were playing with water pistols.' David didn't want his mother getting him into more trouble by complaining to Johnno's parents or the principal.

'Will you ever grow up?' His mother examined the inside of his shirt collar roughly. 'You'll have to put on a dry vest and shirt before you eat.'

'I'm all right,' David objected, glaring at Darren and Emma who were peeping out the lounge door.

'No, you're not all right.' His mother pushed him towards the stairs. 'I'm not having you getting a cold and missing school. Now I'll have to wash and dry those before morning – as if I didn't have enough trouble already with my sprained ankle . . . '

CHAPTER 3

With a heavy heart, David trudged up to the bedroom he shared with Darren, his eleven-year-old brother. Emma, who was twelve, had a bedroom of her own. When his father was alive David used to sleep in what was now the guest bedroom but that was reserved for Doug whenever he stayed overnight. He couldn't understand what his mother saw in that fellow, apart from his muscles. Compared to someone like his father, Doug was a big ape.

As he was removing his shirt a folded sheet of paper in the pocket caught his attention. It was a Form One which Blitzer, the maths teacher, had given him for having no homework done and not having a textbook. His mother would hit the roof when he asked her to sign it. Nervously he chewed his thumb, thinking of Blitzer's reaction if it wasn't signed in time: 'Byrne, how am I supposed to teach you if you won't make an effort?'

No sooner had he thought this than the image of a darkened classroom floated into his mind. Two fellows wearing balaclavas were prising open the metal cabinet in the corner with a large screwdriver. He knew the cabinet was Blitzer's. When the door swung back the thieves removed something and left it on a nearby desk. Then one of them climbed out through the window. Before his partner could follow, the door to the corridor opened, the lights were switched on and Gerry, the caretaker, stood revealed. Immediately, the fellow in the room tackled him. While they were struggling, the other thief – who was dressed like a biker in a black leather jacket and trousers – climbed back in. He struck Gerry on the head with the handle of the screwdriver. The caretaker sank to the ground, the balaclava of the thief he had been wrestling clutched in his hand. In the interval before the lights were switched off again, David recognised Nick Campbell. He also saw a plastic cake box full of bank notes on the desk near the locker. When the lights went out the vision ended.

David felt dazed. What should he do? Warn Gerry? Phone the police? Tell his mother? He decided to phone the police but when he went downstairs his mother insisted that he begin eating his dinner at once. She wanted to have the kitchen free when Doug arrived.

Wolfing down his sausages and baked beans, David tried to ignore Darren and Emma, who kept arguing about whose turn it was to wash the dishes. Doug strode in while they were having dessert and immediately took charge, sitting at the head of the table with his jumper sleeves pushed up. He had a broad, red face, close-cropped ginger hair and keen, blue eyes. David couldn't help looking at the tattoos on his arms: snakes, an eagle, a dagger and a heart with 'Mam' written across it. His mother was acting like a schoolgirl, smiling at everything he said and putting on a teasing accent. David gulped down the last of his rice pudding and got up to go.

'Aren't you going to help with the washing-up?' Doug asked in his deep, manly voice.

'It's not my turn,' David pointed out, 'and, anyway, I've homework to do.'

'Oh, come now.' Doug petted Tiger, the cat, who, contrary to his usual practice, did not bite him. 'At least you can dry up.'

'Go on, David,' his mother coaxed, backing Doug up.

Hiding his annoyance, David took the towel and dried up after Emma. As if on purpose, Emma seemed to take a year over every dish but finally the last one was put away in the cupboard. Without a word, David left the kitchen, where his mother and Doug were lingering over tea and cake.

Afraid that Darren or Emma might eavesdrop if he used the hall phone, he slipped out the front door and, accompanied by Tiger, walked to the kiosk at the edge of Meadow Park Estate. It was empty. Quickly he dialled 999. The man who took his call listened to what he had to say, then asked his name.

'What does my name matter?' David tried to ignore Tiger, who had squeezed under the door and was rubbing against his legs.

'You're telling me that thieves have broken into Lisheen Post Primary and attacked the caretaker,' the man said in his rough country accent, 'but you refuse to give me your name.'

'All right then,' David conceded. 'This is the Salmon.' Before he could say more the man at the other end cut him off.

'What will I do now?' he asked Tiger. It was obvious that the police operator thought it was a hoax call. Maybe

28

the *Lisheen Leader* – or the 'Lisheen Liar', as Doug called it – would take him seriously. He phoned directory enquiries and got the *Leader's* number. Signalling to Tiger to stay quiet, he dialled the newspaper. A girl answered. He told her what he had told the police operator, adding that he was the Salmon. The girl told him to stop playing silly tricks and hung up.

Next day the school was agog with the news that the caretaker had been attacked and was now in hospital. A rumour grew that drug addicts were responsible. Nick Campbell acted as upset as the other pupils. How could anybody do such a horrible thing to a nice guy like Gerry? his face seemed to say. Blitzer's room was kept off limits till the police could inspect it for clues and fingerprints. Billy told David and a crowd of girls that in his High School in New York the security guards were armed and before he left, one had been shot dead by a teenage drug gang.

'Did you see it happen?' Rebecca's eyes were as big as saucers.

'You bet,' Billy assured her. 'I was playing basketball when they popped him.'

'Blowing again, Yank,' Johnno jeered as he strolled by with Mack and Muller.

'Feeling jealous, Johnno?' Rebecca called after him. Johnno glared at her but said nothing.

'Was anything taken from Blitzer's room?' David forced himself to ask.

Aisling looked at him out of her lovely grey eyes. 'Yes,' she said. 'All the money Miss Cummins had collected from Class 2E for a theatre trip. She takes them for English in Blitzer's room.'

'There must have been at least two hundred pounds,' Sinéad Foley piped up. 'I heard Lisa Cox talking about it. She said that each of them paid seven fifty.'

David was so overwhelmed by the fact that Aisling had answered his question that he couldn't utter another syllable. He dropped his gaze, hardly hearing Billy's account of the tracking down of the security guard's killers.

During French class in Miss Nerney's room an idea occurred to him. If the police didn't arrest Gerry's attackers, he would write a note to the principal, naming Nick Campbell. But suppose his mind had got things mixed up and Campbell wasn't involved? No, if he had got the other details correct that must be correct too. And Lisa Cox, who knew all about the money, was Nick's girlfriend. It all added up. Nevertheless, he decided to wait till the following day before sending the note.

At lunch time he told Billy about Johnno's plan to lure him to the canal on Friday.

'Thanks, man.' Billy pretended to punch him on the arm. 'I owe you.'

'What will I do if you don't turn up?' David asked. 'Not that I want you to turn up – you know what I mean?' he added quickly.

'Have you ever thought of joining a gang?' Billy spoke in a low voice.

'We don't have gangs,' David pointed out.

'Then we'll form our own.' Billy accompanied him to the edge of the pitch where a crowd of boys in their school uniforms were playing Gaelic football. 'We could call ourselves the Warlords.'

'What about the Kelts?' David explained that his uncle

used this name for salmon who were returning to the sea. 'Salmon know things we don't,' he added.

'Cool,' Billy agreed. 'Or we could call ourselves the Barracudas. They're great fighters.'

'The Kelts were also great fighters.' David changed tack.

'Okay,' Billy smiled, 'the Kelts it is. We'll work out the details later. Now give me the low-down on this here game. It sure as hell ain't football.'

CHAPTER 4

On Friday evening David walked nervously along the canal path. He had tried time and again to foresee what would happen when Johnno and his mates found that he had come without Billy but nothing had appeared, not even the vaguest image. Could it be that his power had gone? It never seemed to work when he wanted it.

A waterhen flying into reeds growing along the bank startled him. Nervously he chewed on his thumb, thinking of Johnno's sneering face as he warned, 'Be there at six, or else . . .'

Clear as daylight he saw the punks halting by a red MG. Mack pretended to tie his lace while he pushed something under the rear wheel. Then he rose and the punks moved casually away.

Deciding not to wait a moment longer, David hurried to Pine Lawns Estate. Mrs Jones' red MG was parked on the street outside a semidetached, two-storey house. One glance showed a loaf wrapper lodged under the outside rear wheel as if blown there by the wind. Hesitantly he rang the door bell.

'Is Billy in?' he asked the glamorous Black woman who opened the door.

'Oh, yes. Come in,' she invited. 'Billy's upstairs, setting up his darkroom equipment. You're David, I guess?'

'Yes,' David nodded.

'I'm Janet, Billy's mom,' Mrs Jones beamed, playing with a button on her expensive-looking red dress. 'Just wait a moment and I'll let Billy know you're here.'

Returning, she led David into the sitting room and brought him a glass of lemonade and a plate of muffins, chatting all the time about Lisheen and how different it was from New York.

'You're fortunate to live in a nice town like this,' she told him. 'Everybody is so friendly.'

David was about to mention the loaf wrapper he had seen under the car wheel but instead asked about her work in Compu-Tel.

'I'm a training supervisor in the Integrated Products Division,' she explained. 'Once the staff are fully trained I'll be sent to Phoenix, Arizona. It's very challenging work. What do your parents do?'

'Well, my father's dead.' David examined his finger nails.

'Oh, I am sorry,' Mrs Jones said. 'How tactless of me.'

'He used to work as a draughtsman for Griffin and Sons, the builders.' David found himself responding to the warmth in her voice. 'Then, about three years ago, he got pneumonia. My mother always said he neglected his health.'

'Your mother must have found it difficult to carry on without him.' Mrs Jones held out the plate.

'I suppose so.' David took another muffin. 'She got a

job as a cook in O'Neill's Café, five mornings a week. But she's not working this week because she sprained her ankle.'

'My word, she does have it hard,' Mrs Jones declared. 'And I thought I had problems when my good-for-nothing husband ran off. But as things turned out, he did me a favour. I went to night classes and landed a job as a computer analyst in Chase Manhattan Bank. From there, it's been all uphill. Yes, education was definitely my lifeline. Which reminds me – I see that the caretaker in your school is out of danger. It's in the *Lisheen Leader*. Now where did I put it?'

She located the paper under a pile of magazines and showed David the front page. Alongside an article about the spread of drug abuse to the suburbs, there was another with the headline: 'CARETAKER RECOVERS FROM ATTACK.' Further down there was a subheading: 'Who is the Salmon?'

Taking the paper, David read that the gardaí wanted the person who had phoned before the break-in to contact them again. If he did so, his identity would be kept confidential. The writer went on to reveal that the person calling himself the Salmon had also been in touch with the *Leader*. Unfortunately, the caller had hung up before the receptionist could find out whether or not he was a prankster.

While David was marvelling at this barefaced lie, Billy came downstairs with a camera.

'Hi, cara,' he addressed David with the Gaelic word for 'friend' which the Kelts had adopted as their greeting. 'Mind if I take a photo of you and Mom? I want to try out this new lens.'

34

David nodded and posed, grinning, with Mrs Jones while Billy flashed away.

'I'll have to get on with my work now,' Mrs Jones excused herself. 'Call round any time you feel like it.' She gave David a hug.

'Your mam's nice,' he told Billy when Mrs Jones went out.

'Yeah, Mom's the greatest,' Billy agreed. 'Did you go to the canal?'

David nodded, adding that the punks hadn't turned up. Then he mentioned what he had seen under the car wheel. They went out and Billy picked up the wrapper. Inside there was a block of wood with six-inch nails sticking up from the top.

'If your mam had driven over that it would have wrecked the tyre,' David said. 'I'll bet it was Johnno's lot that did it. They probably never intended to go near the canal; they just wanted you out of the way.'

'You're probably right.' Billy replaced the wrapper and put the block back under the wheel. It was now past sunset and the light was fading. Quickly he took two flash photos, then, handing the camera to David, he instructed him to take a photo of him holding the exposed block in one hand and the wrapper in the other.

'Why did you want me to do that?' David returned the camera.

'Evidence.' Billy smiled grimly. 'Those guys sure are mean punks. But I'll make them pay for this. Do you think it was them that mugged the caretaker?'

'No,' David shook his head. 'Can I tell you a secret?'

'Yeah, sure.' Billy put on the lens cap. 'Let's go inside. But don't breathe a word of this to Mom.' He indicated the wrapped-up nail block, which David was now holding. 'I don't want her worrying.'

Back in the sitting room Billy listened open-mouthed to David's account of his visions.

'And you swear this is on the level?' he finally asked.

'Yes.' David pointed at the *Leader*. 'Do you see there where they mention the Salmon? That was me that phoned them.'

'You've got to be kidding.' Billy skimmed the article.

'No,' David assured him.

'Can you call up a vision now, here, this minute?' Billy laid down the newspaper.

'I can try,' David said, 'but it doesn't always work.' He chewed his thumb, trying to visualise the punks as he did so.

'Well?' Billy demanded.

'No luck,' David confessed. 'But I did have a vision on Tuesday of Johnno entering the pawnshop just like I told you. If you don't believe me, come to Dublin tomorrow and we can stake out Barretts on Capel Street.'

'You're on.' Billy picked up the camera. 'And I'll bring this with the telescopic lens fitted. We could make it the Kelts' first job: MISSION OMEGA. By the way, I've recruited two jocks from Third Year: Maurice Quinn and Tom Farrell. They like my style on the court.'

'You're kidding! They're on the under-sixteen football team.' David's eyes lit up.

'They also play basketball.' Billy took a bite out of a muffin. 'We've got real muscle now. We could invite the girls too. You phone Aisling and I'll phone Rebecca and Sinéad.'

'Will you phone Aisling?' David reddened. 'I wouldn't have the nerve.'

'Suit yourself,' Billy shrugged. 'But you won't even get to first base if you act like that.'

'And will you promise not to tell anyone I'm the Salmon?' David went on. 'If the fellow that put poor Gerry in hospital found out, he'd come after me. Even Campbell must be as sore as hell because the police questioned him.'

'Sure,' Billy agreed. 'We're in this together. But you'd better not be spinning me a yarn about your visions. If Johnno doesn't show tomorrow, look out!'

CHAPTER 5

David stood with Billy on a footpath in Capel Street munching an apple. Men, women and children walking by barely glanced at them, though both had on baseball caps, sunglasses and rain jackets. It was Billy's idea that they alter their appearance and with his expensive-looking camera, many people probably dismissed him as a tourist. Since the yellow rain jacket he was wearing was Mrs Jones's and the baseball cap was Billy's, David wasn't sure whether he himself looked like a tourist or a halfwit.

They had spent an hour dawdling along Capel Street and Parnell Street, looking in to shop windows and retreating as far as Virgin Cinemas, from where Barretts pawnshop with its three gold spheres was just visible. The girls, Rebecca, Sinéad and Aisling, had grown tired of waiting and had gone off to Henry Street to do some shopping.

'Are you sure that was the pawn shop you saw?' Billy asked for the hundredth time.

'Yes,' David said, 'but I'm not sure of the day or whether it was morning or afternoon.'

'Listen, man,' Billy rubbed his hands together to warm them, 'I'm out of here. I was nuts to believe your story.' He strode off down Parnell Street without once looking back.

His heart in his shoes, David watched Billy disappear round the corner. Just when he thought he had a friend he had lost him. What use was his second sight if he was doomed to being an outsider all his life? He was on the point of running after Billy when his father's image floated into his mind.

They were at the races in Kilmore and his father was already tipsy. 'Here,' he was saying, 'I won't be needing this,' and he handed David his gold watch. David knew that his dad had been given the watch by Griffin and Sons when he was their top draughtsman and he tried to avoid seeing the pain in his eyes.

'I can't take it, Daddy.' He held out the gift.

'Take it.' His father fitted the strap about his wrist but it was too loose. 'If I keep it I'll only end up pawning it. When we get home I'll make another hole for the buckle.'

David relented. This was to have been a special day out for both of them but every horse his father backed seemed to lose. David watched him getting more and more desperate. It was only later he found out that his father had been laid off the previous day. Giving the watch to him was his way of telling David that whatever went wrong he would always be his favourite. And now Johnno had it.

Without thinking, David began chewing his thumb. Immediately he had a vision of Billy surrounded by the three girls, who were pointing excitedly to the street behind them. They had sighted the quarry. David's heart leaped with a joy that was almost pain. Hurrying down Capel Street he met the others coming out of Mary Street.

Aisling gave him a glad smile and emboldened by his disguise, he smiled back.

'Quick!' Billy cried. 'The punks are on their way!'

The five of them raced up Capel Street, dodging pedestrians, and turning into Parnell Street, stopped by an antique shop, which the girls entered. Billy stayed outside and focused his telescopic lens on Barretts, while David pretended to examine guitars in a music shop across the street.

Within two minutes Johnno and Mack appeared, along with a tough looking older fellow wearing a black leather jacket and trousers. David gasped. Though he hadn't seen him without a balaclava, he could swear that the newcomer was the biker thief who had felled Gerry with the screwdriver. Why hadn't he seen him in the vision of Johnno and his mates walking into the pawnshop? Maybe he had, only he had assumed the third person was Muller? But what was the biker doing here?

Anxiously he chewed his thumb. After a few seconds he saw a counter with vertical bars above it. Johnno and Mack and their biker companion were standing before the counter, while behind it an assistant was examining David's Omega watch. The assistant turned away, went to a back counter and screwed a small viewing piece into his right eye. Then he peered at the watch from different angles. Finally he picked up a scalpel and, prying off the back cover, examined the inside. Satisfied, he replaced the cover and handed the biker a docket and five ten-pound notes.

Back in reality, just at that moment the three punks surreptitiously looked around to make sure that no one was observing them. Luckily for David, the vision dissolved in time for him to duck back out of sight. When he peeped around the corner again, the three had entered the pawnshop. Quickly David slipped across the road to Billy.

'Were you able to snap them?' he asked.

'You bet.' Billy grinned. 'Five perfect shots. Now I've only to get them coming out.'

'What if they come down this street?' David said.

'You worry too much,' Billy told him. 'Why don't you and the girls wait for me at the cinema centre?'

'No, it's my watch,' David pointed out. 'You wait with the girls. I'll take the photos.'

'Fine.' Billy handed him the camera. 'It's focused already. All you have to do is click and wind on. And if you see them coming, make tracks.'

Ages seemed to pass before the three re-emerged. David caught them square in the viewfinder and pressed the release. He was about to take a second photo when he saw Johnno looking in his direction. At once he turned and, controlling his panic, strolled away. He could sense that the three were close behind him. Every moment he expected to hear a shout and the skittering of feet. Increasing his pace, he pressed on. Sweat beaded his forehead and his heart pounded in his chest. Nevertheless, his disguise must have worked because when he crossed the street into the cinema foyer, nobody followed.

Billy and the girls were waiting.

'You were fantastic!' Aisling enthused.

'Don't turn around,' Billy warned, looking through a glass door. 'They're walking along the far sidewalk. Did you get a good shot?'

'Yes.' David removed his baseball cap. 'Phew! That was close,' he added dramatically.

41

Giving Johnno, Mack and the biker enough time to pass beyond viewing distance, the five Kelts trooped over to Barretts. The pawnbroking department was downstairs.

'Yes?' the middle-aged assistant barked from behind the counter.

'I'm looking for an Omega watch.' David took off his sunglasses.

'Can't you read?' the man pointed to a notice on the wall: 'NOBODY UNDER 18 YEARS SERVED'.

'This watch was stolen from me by the three fellows who were just in here,' David explained. 'My father gave it to me.'

The man eyed him and his friends suspiciously. Then his expression softened. 'Can you describe the watch?' he said.

David did so and the man went over to a drawer and returned with the Omega watch.

'Yes, that's it.' David reached out.

'Not so fast.' The man held up his hand. 'I accepted this in good faith. Hey stop that!' he yelled as Billy prepared to take a photo. 'What do you think you're doing?'

'Gathering evidence for the cops.' Billy lowered the camera.

'Go ahead,' the man snorted. 'If you want to contact the gardaí I won't stop you. But you'll have to establish proof of ownership. Now, if I had the docket, I could return the watch this instant for the fifty pounds I gave for it. Otherwise, I'm required by law to wait four months before resale.'

'That's it!' Aisling broke in. 'Johnno's crowd don't want the watch back. They're only after the money. I'll bet anything they threw the docket away.'

42

'Come on!' Billy cried. 'What are we waiting for?'

The five of them retraced their steps down Parnell Street. They had only gone half a block when Rebecca found the docket lying in the gutter between an orange peel and a broken syringe. Back to the pawn shop they raced. Unfortunately, they had only twenty-four pounds between them.

'Why don't you write down your address, phone number and details of the theft?' the assistant suggested. 'I'll see what I can do. Mind you, I'm promising nothing.'

David wrote out the required information on a sheet of paper, knowing that the watch would be kept till he could reclaim it. Later, strolling through the crowds in Henry Street he felt a mixture of fear and elation. On one hand, he was part of a group that included Aisling, on the other, he might run into Johnno, Mack and the biker at any moment.

CHAPTER 6

'No, I don't have fifty pounds to give you,' David's mother snapped. 'Do you think I'm made of money? You lost the watch through your own carelessness, so you can make do with a digital one.'

'But I don't have any money,' David pointed out, 'and you won't let me get a job. It was the only thing of Dad's I had.'

'That's the truth.' His mother stopped washing the table to glare at him. 'But it's more than he left me. Do you know that there were days when I hadn't a penny to buy food for your dinner? If your Aunt Bernie hadn't helped me out you, Emma and Darren could have starved for all your precious father cared. No, it was the drink that was always his main concern, that and the horses. And you'll end up like him if you begin running off to Dublin with your Yankee friend instead of doing your share of the work – leaving me and Emma to slave about the house and mow the lawn while you play the gentleman of leisure.'

David glanced over at Emma, who, with an angelic expression on her face, was tidying the counter.

'I never ask for money for clothes and runners like other fellows my age.' For once David refused to give up the battle.

'Oh, so first it was the watch; now it's clothes.' His mother's voice rose even higher. 'What's wrong with the clothes you have? Is it designer jeans and shirts you want? What's got into you? You'll be demanding your own chauffeured limousine next. Isn't it bad enough that the McGinleys are selling out? You didn't see the 'For Sale' sign, I suppose? Too busy thinking of clothes and watches.'

'What does it matter who lives next door?' David demanded. 'You never talk to the McGinleys anyway.'

'That's enough of your lip.' His mother raised the dishcloth as if to hurl it at his face. 'Now get up to your bed at once.'

'Can't I even stay and do my maths?' David glared at Emma, who was unable to conceal a grin.

'Do your maths?' his mother lowered her brows. 'Do you take me for an eejit? You mean watch the film.'

'Don't blame me if Blitzer gives me a Form One,' David sulked.

'Upstairs! At once!' his mother shrieked. 'If you stay here arguing, I'll ground you for a week.'

David decided that it was best to retreat. The euphoria he had felt walking around Dublin with Aisling and the Kelts still buoyed him up. He had just picked the wrong time to touch his mother for cash.

As he climbed the stairs he reflected that at least he would have the room to himself. When Doug wasn't around, Darren slept in the guest room, claiming that David's twisting and turning kept him awake.

The treachery of lying between sheets used by the man who was trying to supplant their father didn't seem to bother him.

Switching on the bedroom light David's eye immediately fell on the cuddly animal posters decorating the walls and the threadbare panda resting on his pillow – wouldn't Aisling think him a right twit if she knew about it? With only a moment's hesitation he placed the panda in the bottom drawer of the wardrobe, covering him with a folded blanket. Now that he was a Kelt he didn't need soft toys.

With a light heart he washed his teeth, changed into his pyjamas and turning off the light, slid under the bedclothes. Images of Aisling, her eyes crinkled into a smile, her fair hair glossy as silk, her lips parted over her even white teeth, filled his mind. What was she doing now? Watching TV with her family? Doing homework? Taking a bath? Almost without thinking, he chewed his thumb, eager to find out.

An unfamiliar street with cruising cars and late evening strollers enveloped him. Aisling, dressed in a short dark dress and wearing platform shoes, was walking hand in hand with Tom Farrell. The two of them were chatting and laughing. They turned in the door of a lounge bar with The Red Grouse in neon letters above it. Presently a patrol car drew up and two cops got out. They entered the bar. Then as quickly as it had appeared the scene dissolved.

Sick at heart, David stared into the darkness. What an eejit he'd been, imagining that Aisling was interested in him? She'd probably only been nice to him out of pity. Oh, God, he could die of shame. And to think that she'd two-timed him with Tom Farrell, a fellow Kelt! So much for their secret society. It was all a sham, a child's game. But he wouldn't give either of them the satisfaction of letting on that he knew. Tom Farrell might be a good footballer but he, David, had second sight. Nevertheless, he retrieved his panda from the drawer and cuddling it in his arms, thought of his father who a thousand years ago would sit on his bed telling him a story till he dropped off to sleep. If only his dad were here now . . .

His thoughts were interrupted by a timid knock. Emma came in.

'Do you want a bite?' She walked over to the bed, holding out a bar.

'No.' In the back light from the hall he couldn't see her face clearly. 'I just washed my teeth. What's up?'

'I just wanted to say that Mam shouldn't have gone on at you like that. She was really thick all evening, ever since she got the phone call from Doug. He's on his way to Barcelona.'

'Thanks for telling me.' David was sorry for the hostility he had felt towards her earlier. 'Is the film any good?'

'No, another of those silly love stories that Mam likes. I'm only watching it till the next break. By the way, about an hour ago I saw Johnno and those two creeps he goes around with, trying to coax Tiger. Luckily, Darren came and interrupted them. What do you think they were up to?'

'Who knows?' David tried to blot out the memory of a cat he had seen at the bottom of the canal with a concrete block tied to its neck. 'They probably just wanted to pet him. Did you see the "For Sale" sign going up?'

'Yes. Mam is afraid that someone will buy it and let it out to students, like what happened with Number 8. Then we'll be kept awake with wild parties and loud music.

I think it's super but of course I couldn't tell her that.'

David had heard his mother talking about the owner of Number 8, a man who drove around in battered cars. She was always giving out about absentee landlords.

'Is Darren watching the film?' he asked.

'No, he's playing with his knights and warriors.' Emma turned away. 'I'd better get downstairs before Mam gets suspicious.'

CHAPTER 7

Next day, on his way home from church, David called to Billy's house.

'What got you out at this ungodly hour on a Sunday?' Billy was in the midst of his breakfast.

'I was at nine o'clock Mass.' David accepted a blueberry waffle. 'Is your mam up?'

'No, she's still in bed.' Billy poured out a cup of coffee. 'What's up, cara – is my pronunciation improving?'

'Billy,' David ignored the question, 'I've something to ask, something personal.'

'Fire ahead.' Billy poured milk into David's coffee before tucking into the scrambled eggs on his own plate. David was again struck by how smooth and compact his friend's appearance was: close-cropped curly hair, neat ears, features like polished teak on which the corners have been rounded, even white teeth. His own features were thin and angular and his lank hair was always falling into his eyes.

'Did you ever see Tom Farrell chatting up Aisling?' David got right to the point.

'Oh, so that's why you have the long face.' Billy spoke through his full mouth. 'I did overhear him say something to her on Friday; he was to bring her to this pub where there's great crack – is crack what I think it is?'

'You mean dope?' David shook his head. 'No, it's just a word for fun – having a bit of craic. Was the name of the place The Red Grouse?'

'Could be.' Billy swallowed a mouthful of coffee. 'I remember it had something to do with a beef – a complaint. Say, you didn't have one of your visions?'

David told him about what he had seen in bed the previous evening.

'Do you think it's all over then?' He tried to keep his voice matter of fact. 'My chances with Aisling, I mean.'

'Like hell it's over.' Billy wiped his mouth and pink palms with a paper napkin. 'You don't quit the field just because there's a little competition.'

'Tom isn't little,' David pointed out. 'He's a good athlete and, what's more, he's one of the best looking fellows in the school. I haven't a snowball in hell's chance against him.'

'Hold it!' Billy raised his finger like a teacher. 'Tom may have more body power but you have mental power. It's like the bull and the matador; you have only to relax and keep your nerve – and wham!'

He made a pretence of stabbing David with the fork.

'That's great in theory,' David said, 'but no girl is going to turn her back on a star athlete for the likes of me.'

'Then we'll turn you into an athlete.' Billy laid his hand on David's shoulder. 'Wait here till I wash my face and we'll go out front and practise basketball. I'll teach you some moves I'm going to employ against Kilmore in the semi-final. You'll be as cool as 'Magic' Johnson.'

'I can't.' David rose. 'Mam says I have to do my maths. If Blitzer gives me another Form One, I'm grounded.'

'Bull! You can't let a fascist like Blitzer dictate how you spend your Sundays.' Billy scraped his plate into the bin. 'Isn't it enough that you have to attend Mass?'

'Well, I'll play for ten minutes,' David conceded. 'But honestly, Billy, I'll have to go after that. You don't know my mother when she's mad.'

'You don't have to tell me,' Billy grinned. 'Mom is always on my case about homework assignments: "If you don't study, you'll end up a bum like your old man." Did I tell you that my father was actually elected to Phi Beta Kappa in college? Come upstairs and I'll show you his key.'

'What's Phi Beta Kappa?' David followed Billy up the carpeted stairs.

'An honours society,' Billy said over his shoulder. 'Dad was getting straight A's in City College till his brother, my Uncle John, got killed in Vietnam.'

Billy's room had camera equipment, a ghetto blaster, a laptop computer and various items of clothing lying about and the walls were bright with posters of basketball players and pop stars.

'Your room is fabulous,' David remarked. 'Is that 'Magic' Johnson?'

'No, Michael Jordan.' Billy took a cigar box out of a drawer. 'This is the Phi Beta Kappa key – 14 carat gold. You can see Dad's name on the back: William Jones CCNY 1969. That was the year of the Woodstock festival – you know, Janis Joplin, Jimi Hendrix, Arlo Guthrie, all the great rock and folk singers. Dad was there swilling beer and smoking pot just like the best of them. He's often told me about it.'

'I'd love to visit America.' David took the small golden trinket and examined it closely. What his father's watch meant to him, this meant to Billy. He would never forgive Johnno for what he had done. 'Where's your father now?'

'The last time I saw him he was down in the East Village – that's in Lower Manhattan.' With a wistful expression, Billy replaced the key in the cigar box, which he then put back in the drawer. 'He was working as a night watchman on a building site but I guess that was just a cover for peddling drugs. Dad never managed to shake the habit. Say, Dave,' he suddenly perked up, 'why don't you try to foresee if you and I will ever visit New York together. I could show you the Village and Times Square and Central Park.'

David chewed his thumb but just as he expected, nothing appeared.

'It never works when I want it to,' he complained.

'Maybe you have to lock onto someone's brain waves, like in TV reception,' Billy speculated. 'The stronger the signal, the easier it is to pick it up. Which reminds me— ' He went into an adjoining room and returned with a white envelope. 'These are the photos we took in Dublin. They came out pretty good.'

'They're cool!' David enthused, flicking through the bunch till he came to a clear shot of the biker. 'If we could find out something about this character we would be on our way to nailing Johnno.'

'That's what I was coming to.' Billy let a slow grin spread across his face. 'I was showing these to Mom last night and she's convinced that she's seen the biker at

Compu-Tel. He's either a security guard or one of the delivery men. In either case it's only a matter of time till Mom gets the low-down on him.'

CHAPTER 8

'**W**ell, if it isn't Davina!'

It was Monday morning and Johnno and his sidekicks were standing by the wall at the entrance to Pine Lawns, puffing fags.

'I thought you promised to bring Coco Pops down to the canal on Friday.' Johnno threw his arm across David's shoulder in a way that would appear friendly to passers-by.

'I did,' David lied. 'It was you guys who didn't turn up.'

'You weren't there at seven.' Iggy MacDermott hit him in the ribs with his elbow.

'You said six,' David groaned. 'We waited for ages.'

'You didn't wait long enough.' Jim Mullooly blew a cloud of smoke in his face. 'Will I give him a memory refresher, Johnno?'

'No,' Johnno drawled. 'We'll give him a fine. Three pounds for this first offence.'

'I've only got one-fifty, and it's for my lunch snack,' David objected.

'Hand it over.' Johnno pinched his shoulder. 'You can

give us the rest on Wednesday when you bring Coco Pops to the canal. And make sure it's seven this time,' he added, pocketing the money.

David watched the punks crossing the road to join up with Nick Campbell and a few other hard guys who were dismounting from bicycles. Tears formed in his eyes. It wasn't fair the way Johnno's crowd picked on him. If only he could get Doug to sort them out . . . But the memory of a comment Doug had made to his mother about his small physique still rankled. He would sooner die than ask that big ape for help. The guffaws of the punks added to the mixture of shame and anger that threatened to engulf him.

Chewing his thumb, he saw Campbell standing in the hall of some house. A beefy fellow with a shaven head wearing a leather jacket and dirty jeans, was holding out a small plastic bag filled with tablets. Campbell examined the tablets then he handed the fellow a wad of bank notes. When he had counted the money the skinhead gave Campbell the plastic bag.

'Hi, cara.' Billy's cheery greeting brought him back to reality.

David was delighted to see his friend, though the jeers and catcalls from the opposite footpath were an unpleasant warning of trouble ahead. Ignoring the punks, he told Billy about his latest vision and the Wednesday appointment.

'You're sure it wasn't the biker you saw with the tablets?' Billy's voice was calm, unhurried.

'No,' David assured him. 'This fellow was stockier and dirtier. I never saw him before.'

'If we knew where the house was we could nail those creeps.' Billy smiled and waved at Johnno. 'I reckon the money taken from Blitzer and the fifty pounds from your watch ties in with the deal. The question is: who's Mr Big? It's certainly not Campbell or the biker – or the skinhead for that matter. They're the heavy hitters but they haven't got the smarts for the top job. In a setup like this there are always the punks who do the leg work, the heavy hitters who do the distribution and enforcing – Campbell, I reckon, is moving up from the punks to the heavies – and then there's the top dog, Mr Big, the man.'

In school David learned that Gerry, the caretaker, was out of danger, though still recuperating at home. He saw Aisling and her friends during morning break but aware of what had happened – or was still to happen – between her and Tom Farrell, he avoided her gaze. At lunch time he kept away from the toilet, fearing that the punks might come in after him. As a result, when the bell went he entered Blitzer's room in a state of extreme discomfort.

Blitzer's class was made up of students from the three top streams who were unable for higher level maths, as well as all the students in Class 2D who were considered good enough for ordinary level. Many of the latter, especially the boys, were messers, loud and rough looking. The first thing that David noticed when he passed through the door was that the window had a new pane of glass and there was a metal latch and padlock on the cabinet door. When he sat down he saw a swastika drawn in chalk on the blackboard.

'Silence!' Blitzer strode in, dressed as usual in his white lab coat. 'Silence!' he roared again. 'Get your books open! Byrne, why isn't your textbook out?'

'My mother wouldn't buy one,' David replied. 'She said she'd bought one already.' The class tittered.

'Silence!' Blitzer roared. 'Books open and mouths

closed. You, Byrne, see me at the end of class. How am I supposed to teach you if you haven't got a textbook?'

'Please, sir,' David raised his hand, 'can I go to the toilet?'

'You can, Byrne, but you may not.' Blitzer smiled at his own joke. 'You had the entire lunch break to go to the toilet. O'Rourke, what are you grinning about? Get that stud out of your nose or you'll be bringing me in five pounds. How people expect me to get you lot ready for Junior Cert is beyond me.'

'Are you saying that we're stupid, sir?' O'Rourke demanded.

'No, Master O'Rourke, I'm not saying you're stupid but I am suggesting that some of you are academically challenged.' Blitzer allowed himself another little smile. 'Now that you've finally got your books open would you please do question five while I check your homework. Yes, Miss Redford, question five on page ninety-seven the one after question four – which I'm sure you did over the weekend. Yes, Byrne, what is it now?'

'Please, sir, I have to go to the toilet. It's an emergency.' Desperation gave David courage.

'Tie a string on it,' a stage whisper from the back advised.

'Silence!' Blitzer roared. 'If I hear any more of that kind of talk, I'll make the person responsible wish he'd been born dumb. All right, Byrne. Two minutes max: one minute to go, one to return. And in future use the toilet during the break.'

Burning with shame, David avoided everyone's eyes as he hurried to the door. While walking down the corridor he chewed his thumb and immediately had a vision of

O'Rourke throwing a punch at Blitzer. He wondered if he should return and warn Blitzer but quickly dismissed the idea. Anyway, he couldn't risk flooding the corridor.

While he was in the toilet footsteps approached. Quickly he dived into a cubicle. Two fellows with deep voices came in, demanded his name, and satisfied that he was only a Second Year, proceeded to strike matches. A sweet pungent smell mingled with the reek of disinfectant and urine. Grass, thought David anxiously. If I leave now and they're caught, will they accuse me of snitching on them?

CHAPTER 9

When David returned from the toilet there was an unaccustomed hush in Room 14. Everybody seemed to be hard at work and Blitzer, very pale, was sitting at his desk, writing. He did not even look up when David entered. Making his way to his own desk, he noticed that O'Rourke was gone – Blitzer had probably sent him to the principal.

Joe Burke passed him over his textbook and he wrote down questions 5 and 6 before passing it back. While he was trying to figure out how to solve an inequality, there was a polite knock at the door and in answer to Blitzer's invitation, two cops entered. One of them was Garda Noel Morrison, a friendly man with a little black moustache, the other a good-looking woman with short, fair hair whom he introduced as Garda Sheila Gately. Both carried their peaked caps in their hands.

Noel Morrison told them that he and Sheila had come to talk to them about the crime that had taken place in this very room. As they already knew, Gerry Flynn had been viciously assaulted while attempting to prevent a burglary and was lucky to have survived. Somebody in the school had information that was vital to the solving of this case and if he contacted either himself or Garda Gately he could be sure of absolute confidentiality. Were there any questions?

Vicki Hoare put up her hand to ask if the person he was referring to was the Salmon?

'That's correct.' Noel fingered his moustache. 'If he prefers to use that name that is okay with us. Any other questions?'

'Is there a reward?' Joe Burke piped up.

'I'm afraid not,' Noel smiled. 'Maybe Mr Neary would know if the school has any plans along those lines?"

'Possibly,' Blitzer pondered. 'While doing one's duty should be its own reward, I'm sure that if any student comes forward with information, Mr Keane, the principal, will be eager to show his gratitude.'

'There you have it.' Noel smiled again. 'Now Sheila would like to say a few words to you.'

Garda Gately told them that there was a big upsurge in the use of illegal substances in the town. Some parents had complained about fellows approaching their children in Main Street as they walked home from school. Now, the police didn't want to be seen as spoilsports but contrary to what they might have heard, so-called recreation drugs were extremely dangerous; the use of cannabis – 'hash' or 'grass' – could lead to anxiety and paranoia and the use of ecstasy – 'E' or 'E-tabs' – could lead to death, especially for diabetics. Dealers in the city had even begun to sell heroin with ecstasy in so-called 'party packs'. Students were to inform their parents or teachers if they saw anybody peddling drugs. The taboo on snitching only played into the hands of the dealers. 'Yes, you have a question?' She pointed to Carol Redford.

'Are teachers allowed to search students' bags, on the off-chance that they might find something?' Carol spoke defiantly.

'I think you should address that question to Mr Neary.' Sheila gave her a beaming smile.

'But you're the law,' Carol persisted.

'Then I would say that, depending on the circumstances, they are.' Sheila glanced at Noel, who nodded confirmation.

After the gardaí left, David wondered if he should ignore Blitzer's instruction to see him at the end of class. Deciding that it was better to play it safe, he waited behind.

'Well, what is it?' Blitzer looked at him preoccupied.

'You told me to see you, sir,' David reminded him.

'Oh, yes, yes.' Blitzer opened his drawer and removed a dog-eared textbook. 'Take good care of this; I want it back as soon as you get one of your own. Now make sure you do your homework.'

David thanked him.

Joe Burke was waiting for him outside. 'You don't know what you missed, Byrne,' he began. 'O'Rourke nearly flattened Blitzer. He refused to let Blitzer see what he was hiding in his bag and when Blitzer went to search it, he drew out and hit him – right across the jaw. Pow! Blitzer staggered back. It was wicked!'

'And what happened then?' David was anxious to get to his technical graphics class.

'Oh, the usual.' Joe grinned. 'Blitzer marched him down to Timmy's office. I'll bet he had speed taken. Why else would he take on Blitzer? This school is getting cooler every day!'

'What are you two gabbling about?' Blitzer stuck his head out the door. 'Be off to your classes at once!'

Billy had a note for David when they met in the Main Hall at four o'clock. Impatiently he opened it and read:

Hi David,
Why didn't you speak to me at the break?
Have I done something to make you mad at
me? I'm writing this in Colette's French class
so must hurry.
Aisling.

So she was playing the innocent even while she was going out with Farrell! Well, he could play her at her own game.

'Is it good news?' Billy enquired over the chatter of students converging on the front door.

'Just that she wonders why I didn't talk to her.' David put the note in his shirt pocket next to his heart. That was the first time a girl had ever written to him and while he did not regard it as sincere, nevertheless he would treasure it. 'Is your mam going to pick you up?' He tried to hide his confusion.

'Yeah.' Billy waved at some girls who were waiting to talk to him.

'About the Kelts,' David suddenly remarked, 'I don't think we should meet openly in the school. The less people see us together, the less they will suspect that we have our own organisation.'

'Fine.' Billy walked over to the girls. Now he probably thinks that I don't want to be seen with him, David thought and suddenly he felt like crying.

CHAPTER 10

The sun had set by the time David and Billy reached the towpath beside the canal on Wednesday evening. In the declining light the street lamps on the road above were flickering into life and the town had that serene look which follows rush hour. Without halting they walked along as if out for a stroll.

'You're sure you didn't get any glimpse of this evening's showdown?' Billy scanned the whitethorn hedge that bordered the towpath on the left.

'No, I only saw what I told you.' Nervousness made David's voice sharp. 'There was this cider party down by the railway station and afterwards Johnno, Mack and Muller kicked in a phone box. Then they twisted capstones from a garden wall and smashed young trees along Meadow Park Drive.'

'Are you sure it wasn't in our estate?' Billy asked. 'Our trees are smaller than yours.'

'The street was in semi-darkness but I'm almost certain it was ours.' David felt his stomach muscles tighten at the memory.

'Don't turn around,' Billy warned. 'I think the jackals are on the trail. We've got to lure them up to the fir trees – that's where the gang agreed to wait.'

'Suppose they're delayed?' David strained his ears for the sound of footsteps.

'Then we'll just have to play for time.' Billy's voice betrayed his nervousness. 'Trust me, cara, and you'll be wearing stripes,' he added with attempted bravado.

The sound of footsteps was now distinctly audible and they quickened their pace. They were within a hundred and fifty yards of the fir trees when Johnno hailed them.

'What's your hurry, fellas?' he shouted. 'Not anxious to meet us?'

'Keep going!' Billy hissed. It was all David could do to stop breaking into a run. His stomach felt queasy and his palms were moist.

'Do you think they're in love, Muller?' Johnno's mocking voice sounded as if he were right behind them.

'They could be,' Muller guffawed. 'Billy and Davina: it has a nice ring to it.'

'Why aren't you holding his hand, Coco Pops?' Mack jeered. 'After yesterday's win over Kilmore, you're our new basketball hero and the hero always gets the pretty girl.'

'I thought you said we were just going for a quiet walk to Esker Lock?' Billy said to David in a voice loud enough to carry to their pursuers.

'Did you hear that?' Muller remarked. 'They want to be on their own. Will we leave them, fellas?'

'Leave two lovebirds on their own?' Johnno sounded shocked. 'Where's your chivalry? Suppose someone attacked them?'

'You're welcome to join us if you like,' Billy called over his shoulder.

'That's very nice of you, Yank.' Johnno moved up alongside David, while Mack walked beside Billy and Muller dogged their heels.

'Why are you in such a hurry, Davina?' Johnno put his arm around David's shoulder. 'Are you feeling nervous?'

'No.' David's mouth was so dry he almost croaked.

'Then ease it up a bit,' Johnno advised. 'This ground is a bit uneven'.

'So what do you think of the Emerald Isle, Yank?' Mack nudged Billy with his elbow.

'Oh, it's fine,' Billy spoke quietly. 'Of course you do get racists here just like you do in the States.'

'Are you implying we're racists?' Johnno's voice had a menacing edge.

'No,' Billy assured him. 'Most racists are cowards: they only pick on people who are weaker than themselves or that they outnumber. You guys wouldn't do that.'

'We might if it was necessary to keep them away from our girls,' Johnno said. 'I've noticed you attract women the way a pile of horse dung attracts flies.'

'You mustn't have much respect for these girls if you compare them to dung flies,' Billy observed easily.

'You've a very smart mouth, Coco Pops.' Johnno pulled David out of the way and stepped in close to his intended victim.

'You told me that before,' Billy remarked.

'I'll do more than tell you.' Johnno crouched like a boxer and put up his fists. 'Come on, blackie.'

'What's dis, my man?' Billy switched into jive talk.

'It's your funeral, smart ass,' Johnno sneered.

'Speak to de hand, de face ain't listenin',' Billy lilted, ducking aside as Johnno charged.

'Wait!' David cried. 'There's somebody coming.'

At that moment Maurice Quinn and Tom Farrell emerged from the fir trees with Rebecca and Aisling. To David's chagrin Aisling was hanging on to Tom's arm while Rebecca had her arm about Maurice's neck.

'Is this a set up?' Johnno recovered his balance.

'No,' David assured him.

'Well, Coco Pops, it looks as if your buddies have arrived in the nick of time.' Johnno lowered his fists.

'Hi, fellas,' Tom called out. 'Is anything the matter?'

'Come on,' Johnno turned to Mack and Muller. 'We'll settle this another day.'

'Goodbye, boys,' Maurice called out to the retreating punks. 'Mind you don't fall into the canal.'

'Wow, am I glad you guys showed when you did,' Billy confided, grinning at Rebecca.

'We were waiting for you to reach the trees,' Rebecca explained. 'The fight broke out too soon.'

'You'll have to be on your guard from now on,' Tom warned. 'Those three are treacherous gits.'

'Are you okay?' Letting go of Tom's arm, Aisling smiled at David.

'Yeah, sure.' Conscious of her beauty, her total physical difference to his own unattractive self, he was becoming tongue-tied.

'You didn't answer my note.' She looked at him out of her shining grey eyes.

'No,' he mumbled lowering his gaze. Then sick at heart he joined the others, who were debating whether or not to walk to the lock.

CHAPTER 11

David and Billy were using Mrs Jones' computer to design a notice. It was Friday evening and Mrs Jones had left them on their own while she got ready for a trip to the theatre. After numerous false starts they settled for the inscription:

Thrashed by
John Cox, Iggy MacDermott and Jim Mullooly,
Demolition Experts.

Under it they drew the outline of a salmon by having two arcs overlap to form the head and the tail. If David's earlier vision was true, the punks would be exposed.

'Wow! That will freak them out,' Billy declared. 'We'll put six of those on one sheet and then cut them out.'

'I have something to ask you, David.' Mrs Jones came downstairs in a blue dress, with gold rings hanging from her ears and a string of pearls about her neck. 'Why is the Institute of Technology called 'The College'?'

'It used to be the Regional Technical College.' David was pleased to be consulted like a grown-up.

'Oh, thank you.' Mrs Jones sprayed perfume on her neck and behind her ears. 'It's just that my date is a lecturer in the engineering department and I don't want to appear dumb.'

'You look fabulous, Mom.' Billy helped her into her coat.

'Thanks.' Mrs Jones gave Billy and David a quick hug. 'I feel like Cinderella,' she confided as the door bell rang.

When he returned from the window where he had watched his mother and her date drive off, Billy struck his forehead with the heel of his palm.

'That reminds me,' he said. 'Mom got a fix on the biker. He lives in this estate, just in the next block. I've got the number written down somewhere. Will we check him out?'

'No, let's run off the copies first.' David was impatient to begin.

They ran off four copies on the printer and Billy cut them into separate notices. While snipping away, he began reminiscing about a teacher he had in primary school who looked like his mother's date.

'Mike was his name and he was in his late forties. Mike Gilmartin. He used to tell us stories about his school days in Ireland – he never lost his brogue – how some of the priests would flake them if they didn't know their lessons. It was like something from the Deep South – Simon Legree whipping the slaves.'

'What county was he from?' David asked.

'Don't know.' Billy shook his head. 'Somewhere in the west. To hear him talk about it, the place was like Injun Territory, beautiful and underdeveloped. He used to play

'The West's Awake' on the violin and every St Patrick's Day he'd march up Fifth Avenue to 86th Street and come in next day with one hell of a hangover: "All right, boys and girls, open yer books and not a meg or geg out of ye or I won't be responsible for me actions." I was very fond of Mr Gilmartin. Which reminds me – what happened to the guy that hit Blitzer?'

'Niall O'Rourke,' David grinned. 'He got suspended for a week. It seems that Blitzer interceded for him, otherwise Timmy would have expelled him. How will we stick these up?'

'How about Sellotape?' Billy picked up one of the notices.

'No,' David decided. 'We'll use those sticky tabs that teachers use to hang up posters.'

'Fine,' Billy agreed. 'And we'll get the girls to help us – you and Aisling and me and Rebecca. That will work out at six notices each.'

'I'd prefer to stick up my own.' David tried to keep Aisling's face out of his mind. 'I don't want to draw attention.'

'Suit yourself,' Billy shrugged. 'Of course you realise your performance on the court is starting to impress the girls: they reckon you're a future Michael Jordan.'

'Some performance!' David snorted.

'That's not what Aisling thinks.' Billy spoke gently. 'But to get back to the notices. The punks may not do anything – in which case we've gone to all this trouble for nothing.'

'If they don't do it tonight, they'll do it tomorrow night,' David assured him. 'We'd better put these up early in the morning so we won't be seen. Now let's check out the biker.'

They walked around to the address Mrs Jones had traced, 34 Manor Drive, and found a new semidetached house with a Toyota car and two motorbikes parked in the driveway.

'It looks like we hit pay dirt,' Billy remarked.

While they were walking away they heard a motorbike starting up behind them. Quickly they turned the corner but before they had gone twenty yards the motorcyclist, clad in black leather, sped past. Since he was wearing a helmet they could not be sure it was the same man they had seen in Dublin with Johnno and Mack.

Despite his good intentions, it was almost half past eight the next morning before David managed to leave the house. Luckily, nobody was astir. Just as he had seen in his vision, the punks had done a thorough job. Both capstones had been removed from the piers of the garden wall, his mother's standard rosebush was uprooted, newly opened daffodils were strewn across the driveway and the 'For Sale' sign from Number 11 was stuck in the lawn.

As he walked down the street he found that half a dozen saplings had been broken, licence plates had been removed from cars, dustbins were overturned, and more capstones were missing from walls and piers. At the worst spots he pressed a notice into place as if he were casually touching a branch or wall top with his fingers. When he rounded the block he found that the lower glass pane of the phone box had been kicked in and the receiver ripped from its metal cord. He must have slept like a log not to have heard the racket. Nipping inside, he stuck his last few notices onto the upper pane of the phone box. As he did so, an unexpected 'miaow' almost made his heart jump into his mouth. It was Tiger, who had come up to greet him.

Two policemen called to the house while he was having breakfast with Darren, Emma and his mother.

'Do you know anything about this?' Garda Morrison held out the notice when Mrs Byrne had finished accusing him of allowing people to be terrorised in their homes.

'How should I know?' Mrs Byrne fumed. 'You're the gardaí. David, aren't those fellows in your school?'

'What fellows?' David examined the notice before handing it back to Garda Morrison. 'They could be Third Years, I suppose.'

'And do you know anybody who calls himself the Salmon?' Garda Morrison gave him a warm smile.

David shook his head.

'You're sure?' Garda Morrison persisted.

'Of course he's sure,' Mrs Byrne snapped. 'Now good-day, gentlemen.'

CHAPTER 12

It was Sunday before David was able to visit Billy. He had spent most of Saturday helping his mother find the capstones and cement them back in place. While they were returning the 'For Sale' sign to Number 11, they found a 'SOLD' sticker that had been ripped off it. This discovery put his mother into an even worse mood. If she had the money, she grumbled, she would sell out like the McGinleys and move to a civilised area where people's homes weren't vandalised in the night. She hadn't mentioned it before, but Darren had been approached by a skinhead outside the Boys' National School. What sort of a town was it where children were targeted by drug pushers?

'What did the skinhead look like?' David enquired.

'How should I know?' his mother snapped. 'Some dirty lug with his hair shaved off, I suppose. Now hold this upright while I put a few stones around it.'

Billy's mother was even more distraught than his own. 'I had such a lovely time on Friday night,' she explained, 'and then to wake up on Saturday and find 'GO HOME

NIGGERS' sprayed on the gable wall. And Billy tells me they wrote on the 'Help Wanted' notice outside the Chinese restaurant, 'MUST HAVE SLANTED EYES'. Aren't they aware that the 'know-nothings' in my country used to call the Irish 'the filthy outcasts of Europe' and that the employers in New York put up notices, 'NO IRISH NEED APPLY'? Oh, it makes me so angry.'

'Mom's right about the 'know-nothings',' Billy said. 'Mr Gilmartin used to tell us all about them and about 'shanty Irish' and 'lace-curtain Irish'.'

'Who were they?' David looked puzzled.

'Shanty Irish were the dirt-poor Irish that lived in shanty towns,' Billy told him. 'Lace-curtain Irish were the better off ones that could afford lace curtains for their windows. Mr Gilmartin said that for the Irish to practise discrimination when they suffered so much from it themselves was the height of perversity – those were his very words, the "height of perversity". Now look what they've done to my mom.'

'They attacked our house too.' David recounted the damage done and how upset his mother was.

'Oh, I know you're not to blame,' Mrs Jones gave him a hug. 'Most people here have been so welcoming – I shouldn't let a few know-nothings get to me. Billy, fix some pancakes and maple syrup for David. I had a friend bring me maple syrup over from New York, then I found it's sold right here in the supermarket. Seems to me everywhere I look I find something American.'

'Did you put up the notices?' David asked Billy when they were alone in the kitchen.

'You betcha!' Billy grinned. 'Rebecca and I found a whole lot of young trees broken on this estate and down in

73

the Square and we stuck a notice on every one – well, almost every one. The punks must have been on acid or speed to have covered so much territory.'

'Maybe they didn't do all of it,' David pointed out.

'Ah, what the heck!' Billy poured maple syrup plentifully on the hot pancakes. 'If they wrote the stuff on our wall, they deserve whatever they get. By the way, Rebecca wanted to know about the fish logo under the notice so I said it was to hoodwink the punks into thinking the Salmon was on their trail. I didn't tell her you were the Salmon.'

'Thanks.' David held a forkful of dripping pancake poised over his plate. 'The only person I want to know is you.'

'Not even Aisling?' Billy licked his fingers.

'Especially not Aisling,' David declared.

Johnno and his sidekicks surrounded David before he reached the canal bridge the following evening.

'Was it you that put the cops on to us?' Johnno demanded.

'For what?' David looked surprised.

'Stop playing the innocent!' Mack gave him an elbow in the ribs. 'Was it you that accused us of thrashing your estate?'

'Why should I do that?' David groaned. 'Nobody knows who did it.'

'Fine,' Johnno spoke mildly. 'We're going for a nature walk.'

The four of them marched in silence along the towpath for what seemed hours, David getting more nervous as they got further from the town. At last they came to Esker

Lock, a dark, sinister pit with water flowing under a massive wooden gate into a rectangular basin that was closed on the far side by another gate. The sheer cut-stone sides were covered with slimy moss above the water surface, so that there was no chance of a drowning person getting a handhold. Despite himself, David felt his knees shaking violently.

'Stand the prisoner on the gangplank,' Johnno commanded, and Mack and Muller forced him to the brink of the lock.

'Now look down,' Johnno ordered. David tried to look away but Muller bent his head forward with his hand.

'OK, Davina, listen carefully.' Johnno's voice remained even. 'Somebody told me that it was you who shopped us to the cops – you and that darkie friend of yours. No, don't interrupt,' he snapped, as David croaked a denial. 'I'm just going to point out that if you do get us in trouble there could be an accident.'

As he said this Mack and Muller kicked David's feet from under him so that suddenly he was dangling by his arms. David yelled in terror but his eyes were focused on the water far below. How deep was it? Was there mud under the surface? If he managed to swim to the far end would he be able to grab the crossbeam at the bottom of the gate?

'All right!' Johnno's voice interrupted his thoughts. 'That'll do.'

Immediately Mack and Muller yanked him back onto firm ground. Despite the chilly breeze David found he was perspiring.

'Listen, Byrne,' Johnno gripped his shoulder, 'we only want to find out who's spreading these rumours about us.

Chances are it's Coco Pops. If we had that talk on Wednesday as we planned none of this trouble would have happened. Look at it from our point of view. Ever since he came you've been crossing us. Tell the truth and we'll protect you. Is he the Salmon?'

'No, he isn't,' David shook his head. 'He's just an ordinary bloke like me who wants to be left alone.'

'If he wants to be left alone, he'll have to show respect.' Johnno nodded to his sidekicks and without a backward glance, the three of them strode away whistling.

CHAPTER 13

'And this note is from your English teacher?' Doug was presiding at the dinner table like a judge in a courtroom.

'How could I do Tubby's homework when I don't have the book?' David grumbled.

'Couldn't you have borrowed a book from your Yankee friend?' Mrs Byrne took the Form One from Doug. 'You certainly spend enough time in his house. It also says here that you were "inattentive".'

'It seems to me,' Doug sucked his teeth reflectively, 'that the trouble lies with the damn school. Now hear me out, Joan.' He held up his hand to silence Mrs Byrne, who was about to interrupt. 'We can talk till we're blue in the face but the fact of the matter is David isn't making a go of it. You yourself said that his Christmas report was a disaster: "not working to capacity", "doesn't try hard enough", and so on. Nothing whatever about the poor teaching.'

David glared, mortified, at Darren and Emma, who were smirking.

'Couldn't we discuss this later?' Mrs Byrne frowned at her two youngest children.

'No, Joan.' Doug put down his knife and fork. 'We need to deal with this problem head-on. No more shilly-shallying.'

'Well,' Mrs Byrne reddened, 'I've done my best to help him but I can't do anything if his books and equipment keep getting pinched.'

'That's where you're wrong, Joan.' Doug laid his hand on her arm. 'You could take him out of that place where he's mixing with the riff-raff of Lisheen and send him to a proper school like Hollybrook. You said yourself that his friend Jonathan is a boarder there. David could travel up on the bus. What do you say?'

'I don't know.' Mrs Byrne played with the fish fingers and baked beans on her plate. 'I've Darren and Emma to take care of too.'

'I'll cover the extra cost.' Doug looked at her with his masterful expression.

'Why don't you ask me what I want?' David burst out. He had suddenly realised that despite Johnno and his sidekicks, he no longer hated Lisheen Post Primary. The arrival of Billy and his membership of the Kelts had changed everything. Even Aisling's proximity, though it was a torment, was something that he would not be without.

'Whoa there!' Doug scratched his head in perplexity. 'Are you telling us you enjoy being a Bluebottle?'

'I do.' David avoided Doug's eye. 'I'm doing all right at most subjects and I'm almost certain to get on next year's basketball team. Now can I watch television?'

'That's your trouble!' his mother snapped. 'Too much television and not enough studying.'

'I'll do my maths and French after *Home and Away*,' David promised.

'We're just concerned about your future, David.' Doug lit a cigarette and blew smoke through his nostrils. 'A new school might just get you out of your rut.'

'I'd do better if I had all my books,' David pointed out. 'It's not my fault they were taken.'

'Maybe it's not,' his mother agreed. 'However, you wouldn't have things like that happening in Hollybrook; the priests wouldn't stand for it.'

'If I get my books back, can I stay?' David tried to keep his lip from trembling.

'Well, I don't know.' His mother wiped tomato sauce off Darren's face with tissue paper. 'What do you think, Doug?'

'Stop!' Darren protested. 'I'm old enough to clean my own face.'

'We'll give him till after Paddy's Day,' Doug pronounced judgment. 'If you haven't your books by then, David, your mother and I will have to have a chat with that little Hitler of a headmaster, Timmy Keane.'

As he watched television with Darren and Emma, David brooded. It was obvious that his mother and Doug were only looking for an excuse to take him out of the Post Primary. Was it his friendship with Billy that was bothering them? He knew that ever since a group of Nigerian refugees had tried to stow away in his truck, Doug was suspicious of Black people. If only he could meet Billy and Mrs Jones . . .

'Did you see the old battered car parked next door?' Emma asked.

'It's a Volvo,' Darren informed her.

'Mam thinks it belongs to the man who owns Number 8.' Emma lowered her voice. 'She's going to find out who he is so that she can ring him up if there's a wild party. That's why she flipped when she saw your bad note.'

While he fretted over his homework in the dining room, which they used as a study, David's mind wandered to his stolen watch and textbooks. Despite the punks' threat to throw him into the lock, he knew that he had outwitted them. Jokes about 'demolition experts' were flying around the school and somebody had even pasted one of the notices on the trophy cabinet. What were Johnno and his sidekicks doing now?

Chewing his thumb he saw three figures wearing balaclavas appear in a kitchen. While they were ransacking the drawers, Maisie O'Neill, a frail pensioner who lived on her own, confronted them. The raiders pushed her to the ground, unbolted the door and scampered.

Shocked, David wondered when all this was going to happen. He needed more exact information. Concentrating on the punks, he chewed his thumb again. At once he saw them climbing the stairs of the snooker hall. While Johnno and Mack began playing pool, Nick Campbell strode in. He threatened Johnno with a cue stick. The manager came out of his office, whereupon Campbell left, shaking his fist at Johnno.

What could this second vision mean? David's brain felt woozy. It was like having pieces of a jigsaw that didn't fit . . . unless . . . Suppose Campbell was demanding payment for tablets and, in desperation, the punks were going to raid Mrs O'Neill's? Many old people kept cash in their home.

He looked up Mrs O'Neill's number in the phone book but couldn't find it. She probably didn't have a telephone.

Slipping out to the phone box, he dialled 999 and left a message for Garda Morrison, then on impulse he phoned *Crime Stoppers*, who offered rewards for information on crimes. When he told the man who took his call that he was the Salmon, the man told him to grow up.

CHAPTER 14

Father Moore's class was considered a doss. Nobody was interested in religion so he allowed the students to discuss various topics that he selected. Wednesday's topic was 'Young people have too much freedom'. Since almost everybody was violently opposed to this proposition, the more vocal rebels were soon arguing that older people drank, so why shouldn't young people do likewise?

'Don't you drink yourself, Father?' Dermo Campbell, sporting bleached hair, asked.

Father Moore, who was a fun-loving man with a passionate interest in sport, smiled. 'Yes, Dermot. But then I'm over the legal age. I was twenty-four before I indulged.'

'Ah, go on, Father,' Dermo laughed, 'you're only fooling us.'

'I'm not, Dermot,' Father Moore grinned impishly. 'I had my first drink when Dublin won their first All-Ireland – in this decade, I should add.'

'Down the Dubs!' a chorus of voices shouted.

'Keep it quiet,' Father Moore implored. 'Orla, you have

a question?' He indicated Orla Meehan, the class swot.

'You were talking earlier about young people using drugs, but isn't alcohol the most addictive drug in the world?' Orla spoke in a clear, precise voice.

'Yes, Father, what do you say to that?' another girl demanded.

'Why don't I let someone in the class answer?' Father Moore retained his good humour. 'David, so far you haven't made any contribution. Do you think alcohol is an addictive drug?'

David was mortified. Did Father Moore expect him to admit that his father had been a drug addict? 'I don't know,' he hesitated. 'I suppose it could be – but it's not illegal to drink and it is to take drugs.'

'That's only because the government gets taxes from whiskey and beer,' Dermo shouted out.

'David has made a very good point.' Father Moore ignored Dermo. 'Would anybody else like to develop it?'

'Father, don't you think that cannabis – which experts agree is less harmful than alcohol – should be legalised?' Orla fired another shaft.

'Experts also agree that there is a massive difference between cannabis and cannabis resin,' Father Moore pointed out, 'but that's a topic we'll have to leave till another day. To get back to the subject of alcohol: how many of you know what happened at the wedding feast of Cana?' There was an immediate outburst of groans.

'Not another Bible story!'

'Who wants to hear about something that happened two thousand years ago?'

'Who did Cana marry? Abel?'

'Why can't we discuss cannabis?'

Father Moore waited for the protests to die down then he began talking about the ritual connected with a Jewish wedding, how smartly dressed the groom would have been, how beautiful the bride would have looked. Little by little he wove a web of words around his listeners so that even Dermo didn't interrupt.

David couldn't help comparing the bride with Aisling – who now resembled Sinéad O'Connor. What had got into her that she had cut off her lovely hair? It must have been Tom's influence. Billy had told him that the guards had found them drinking in The Red Grouse but because Tom's father was a cop, the whole thing had been hushed up.

'Can you imagine how appalled the parents must have been when they were told that the wine had run out?' Father Moore's voice was working its spell.

'Appalled', that was the only word to describe how he felt about Aisling's haircut. And yet, she did look more striking, in a horrible sort of way. Opening his copybook he scribbled a note.

> *Dear Aisling,*
> *Why did you cut off your lovely hair?*
> *An appalled admirer.*

At morning break he gave the note to Billy to give to her but made him promise not to say who it was from.

'That reminds me,' Billy handed him an envelope. 'Slip these into your pocket. They're photos of the the skinhead and the biker. I snapped them with my telescopic lens.'

While Billy walked over to a mixed crowd of boys and girls who were eager to discuss the school's chances in the basketball county final, which was being played on Friday,

David slunk away to a corner. Would people notice he was again on his own? He wanted to look at the photos but decided it would be too risky.

'Hey, Byrne,' Johnno's voice reached him like the hiss of a snake, 'want to make some money?'

Before he could escape, David found himself hemmed in by the punks.

'Chill out.' Johnno laid a hand soothingly on his arm. 'We're not here to hassle you. How would you like to do both of us a little favour?'

Like the favour you did to Mrs O'Neill? David thought, watching the squinting eyes with horrified fascination.

Johnno took his silence for affirmation. 'Here.' He held out a small plastic bag. 'There are ten E-tabs in this. You sell them at a fiver each and keep ten – no, make that twenty – keep twenty quid for yourself. There'll be no trouble selling them with the St Patrick's weekend disco coming up.'

'What's an E-tab?' David pretended not to know.

'Oh, leave him!' Mack advised. 'He's just a wuss.'

'All right, Byrne.' Johnno pocketed the tablets. 'This conversation never took place. Comprendo?'

'Why don't you ask Billy Jones?' The words tumbled out of David's mouth before he could stop them.

'Maybe we will.' Johnno patted David's cheek then he and his sidekicks drifted away.

David felt as if a steel band was tightening about his forehead. Why had he mentioned Billy? Was it to convince the punks that he wasn't a wuss or to prove to Billy that he wasn't imagining drug deals or maybe even to lash out at him because he had plenty of admirers while he himself had been dumped by Aisling?

Filled with remorse he chewed his thumb. Straight away he saw Billy handing a ten-pound note to Johnno in exchange for two E-tablets.

'No!' he cried aloud, causing a number of students to look in his direction. Ignoring them he went in search of his friend but the bell for class recalled him. Despite a splitting headache he got through the rest of the day without incurring the wrath of any teacher except Blitzer, who marked his homework 'careless'. Fortunately, he only asked David to write out a number of examples instead of giving him a Form One.

CHAPTER 15

When he didn't see Billy at the end of school, David decided to call to his house. Mrs Jones said that Billy had phoned to say that he was going to visit some friends.

'I'll tell him you were looking for him,' she smiled, obviously in a hurry to get back inside.

'Listen,' David blurted out. 'Tell him to be careful.'

'What on earth for?' Mrs Jones raised her eyebrows.

'There's a fellow who may try to sell him drugs,' David mumbled.

'And this fellow's name?' Mrs Jones looked anxious.

'I can't tell you,' David said. 'I just have a feeling.'

'Well, thank you, David,' Mrs Jones looked thoughtful. 'You're a real friend. I imagined this was a problem that we wouldn't face here – in fact, it was one of my reasons for bringing Billy to Ireland. I'm really grateful to you for warning me.'

Feeling like a hypocrite, David turned away. As he walked down the driveway past the red MG he noticed a Volvo parked on the side of the road. It was old and grey and it had a Dublin registration. Was it the same one Emma and Darren had seen outside McGinley's? When he reached Meadow Park Drive the Volvo passed him, then drew to a halt outside Number 8. A respectable-looking man got out and entered the house. If this was the man who had purchased McGinley's, what had he been doing near Billy's house?

David chewed his thumb, trying to visualise the driver of the Volvo. A vision formed and David saw him talking to a man in a pub. The man's face was turned away but there was no mistaking that ginger hair. It was Doug! Crikey, what on earth could it mean? Perhaps nothing. After all, what was so extraordinary about Doug having a drink with somebody who now owned the house next door to his girlfriend's house? The word 'girlfriend' set David's head throbbing again.

Tiger rose to greet him, rolling over on the driveway as David turned in from the road. Stooping, he patted Tiger's head. Quick as lightning a paw shot out, its claws grazing his hand. He looked at the red lines, waiting for the blood to flow. When it didn't, he patted Tiger again, this time avoiding the paw. Pleased, he rang the doorbell.

'What kept you?' his mother demanded.

'Nothing,' David took off his bag. 'Is anything wrong?'

'Yes, something's wrong,' she snapped. 'Darren was offered drugs again by a fellow outside the school and robbers broke into Mrs O'Neill's last night and almost killed her. I don't know what Lisheen's coming to. You should see the crowd that have moved in to Number 11 next door – thugs and addicts by the looks of them.'

'Maybe they're just students from the institute,' David remarked.

'Students my eye!' Mrs Byrne gave a dry laugh. 'But I've found out who the landlord is, a Mr Robinson – the same man who owns Number 8. Mary Cahill in Number 7 told me. She's plagued with the crowd in Number 8 but none of them will tell her where Robinson lives – that is if they know. It seems he comes around in a battered old car to collect the rent, then disappears.'

'Does Doug know him?' David asked in an innocent voice.

'I doubt it.' Mrs Byrne hung up his coat. 'By the way, he phoned to say he won't be coming this evening so you'll have the room to yourself. That should make you happy. Now try to get some homework done before dinner.'

Darren was watching television in the lounge.

'What did the fellow who offered you the drugs look like?' David remained standing.

'How should I know?' Darren was engrossed in a silly cartoon.

'Was it one of these guys?' David showed him Billy's photos.

'That's him.' Darren pointed to the skinhead.

'You're sure?' David pressed.

'Sure I'm sure.' Darren grimaced his annoyance. 'He was giving out half tablets for free. Some of the lads took them. Now can I watch *Spiderman*?'

Three hours later while he was racking his brain over *Invitation au français* in the dining room, David's thoughts wandered to Aisling. He would ask Billy to take a photo of her, which he could carry in his wallet. Would she be going with Tom to the Sunday disco, he wondered.

At first when he chewed his thumb no vision came, then he saw a BMW with its lights on cruising down a lane near the supermarket. The biker was driving and the skinhead and another tough were in the back. The car stopped by a disused warehouse, the lights went dead and the occupants donned balaclavas. At the same time a girl with a shopping bag came walking up the lane. David's blood froze. Despite the semi-darkness, he recognised Aisling. Crikey! Why was she taking the short cut? Next thing, the thugs dashed out of the car and grabbed Aisling.

Controlling his panic, David tiptoed out the door and raced to the phone box. To his dismay there was a woman inside. He hopped about impatiently to attract her attention but she turned her back and continued talking.

Should he run to the other telephone box near the shopping centre? Then he thought of Billy's house. He was about to race off when the woman hung up the receiver. Frantically he dialled 999 and asked for a message to be given to Garda Morrison in Lisheen.

'And where is all this happening?' the woman operator sounded sceptical.

'It's going to happen in the lane behind Lisheen supermarket,' David informed her. 'Tell Garda Morrison that the Salmon told you.'

Next he phoned Billy's home but his mother said that he and his friends had gone to a film in Dublin. In desperation, he dialled directory inquiries and got Aisling's parents' number. When he spoke to her mother she told him that Aisling was getting a few groceries.

David was in a quandary. If he ran to the supermarket he might be too late and if he asked his mother for a loan of her bicycle, she would explode. Deciding that he didn't have any choice, he removed the bicycle quietly from the garage, and peddling like a madman, headed into town. Motorists honked him for cycling without lights but, fortunately, he reached the lane in one piece. The near end was deserted but further down he could see two fellows trying to bundle Aisling into a car. She was struggling and he could hear muffled cries. Ringing his bell furiously, he charged down the lane, shouting, 'Let her go! Let her go!' Pushing her aside, the attackers jumped into the car, which sped off in the direction of Dublin.

CHAPTER 16

'Are you all right?' David jumped off the bike and letting it fall on the ground, raced to Aisling.

'Yes,' she assured him coolly. 'You didn't have to make such a racket.'

David was dumbfounded. What the hell was he supposed to have done? Mind his own business?

'If I had known you would have reacted like this, I wouldn't have bothered.' He walked over and picked up his bike then wheeled it back to her.

'Nobody asked for your help. I can take care of myself.' With her shorn head, her eyes looked enormous.

'That suits me fine.' He threw his leg over the saddle.

'Good.' She picked up the groceries and replaced them in her shopping bag. David preceded her to the end of the lane, cycling slowly.

'What are you waiting for?' she demanded when he halted with one foot on the ground.

'Just making sure you get home okay.' He tried to sound matter of fact.

'I'm okay; thanks for nothing.'

She walked past him into the lighted street just as a patrol car, blue lights flashing, entered the far end of the lane.

'If the police question you, I'd appreciate it if you didn't tell them I was here,' David urged. 'My mother thinks I'm studying.' And then, satisfied that she was now out of danger, he cycled quickly away, the falling rain soaking his hair and jumper.

His mother was furious when he arrived home. What in blazes did he think he was doing, stealing her bike to go cycling in the rain? Had he been visiting his Yankee friend? Well, he could go right up to bed this minute while she tried to dry his clothes for the morning – as if she didn't have trouble enough already. The next time he pulled a stunt like that she would ground him for a year.

Before getting into bed, he stuffed his panda into the drawer. He didn't need him anymore. Aisling's contempt had shown him what a wuss he really appeared to others. Well, he would use his powers as the Salmon to show her and the punks a thing or two.

Why had she been attacked, anyway? Was it because Johnno had set the biker and his pals on her to get even with Tom for turning up at the canal? No matter. He would strike fear into his enemies. But how to do it? The police would, no doubt, question the biker and his pals and then release them for lack of evidence. They must have stolen the BMW and that meant they would have dumped it somewhere. The question was: how would they get home? Of course! They would have left their motorbikes hidden in a convenient spot.

He chewed his thumb but no vision came. Maybe he was too worked up? Never mind! He had an idea. He would send postcards to the biker and his pals and to

Johnno and his sidekicks, supposedly written by an inmate of Mountjoy. Billy could design them on his computer. The cards could say:

> *Looking forward to seeing you inside soon,*
> *Larry the Lag.*

His anger somewhat dispelled by this plan, he tried to sleep, but Aisling's enormous grey eyes seemed to fill the darkness. Why had she been so hostile? And then he knew: it was because he had signed himself 'An appalled admirer'. Dammit, how could he have been so stupid?

Aisling didn't turn up at school next day, neither did Billy.

'Where's Coco Pops?' Johnno demanded during morning break, descending with Mack and Muller on David as he knelt to get books out of his locker.

'I don't know,' David mumbled

'Speak up!' Mack ground his heel into David's toecap.

'You're hurting my foot!' David protested.

'Do you hear that?' Muller picked up a textbook and tossed it to Johnno.

'Is this yours, Byrne?' Johnno let the book drop. Before it hit the floor, David caught it.

'Look, lads,' David spoke in a quiet voice, 'if I lose any more textbooks, my mother is taking me out of this school. In fact, if I don't have the ones I've already lost back by Friday week, I'm gone.' With that he rose from the floor and leaving the books where they were, walked away. Glimpsing the Kelts at the far end of the corridor, he hurried towards them.

'What's up?' Maurice Quinn slapped David's palms with his own as Billy sometimes did.

David told them about the incident at the locker.

'Good for you!' Rebecca gave him an admiring glance. 'Sinéad was just comparing you to Clark Kent.'

'We heard how you rescued Aisling.' Sinéad took a note from her shirt pocket. 'Here, she sent you this.'

'Do you want us to sort out these punks?' Tom gave him a friendly jab.

'Why not?' Almost overcome with emotion, David put the note in his pocket. He would read it later when his mind was calm.

The five walked down the corridor but by the time they reached the locker, the punks had gone. Rebecca and Sinéad knelt beside him on the lino and helped him to replace the books. He smiled his gratitude.

'We have good news for you,' Tom said. 'My old man is a cop and he told me that the BMW was found abandoned outside Kilbride. That means they'll be able to dust it for fingerprints.'

'Did Aisling tell the cops I was there?' David was suddenly fearful that his cover had been blown.

'Not as far as I know,' Tom assured him. 'Why don't you read her note?'

'I will.' David faced the locker to give himself some privacy. The note was written neatly on rose-tinted paper and folded twice.

Hi David,
Sorry I was so awful to you yesterday. Will
explain all when we meet.
A contrite admirer.

Yeeesss! This was going to be a fantastic day!

CHAPTER 17

'What happened?' David surveyed the bruised face of his friend with dismay.

'Come in.'

Billy led the way to the kitchen, where he poured out two orange drinks before slumping in a chair. 'Last night after the film – did Mom tell you I went to the Virgin cinema with Maurice, Sinéad and Rebecca?'

David nodded and sat down.

'Well, on the way back,' Billy continued, 'we went to the chipper here in Lisheen and afterwards I was walking home through the Harbour Field when BAM! somebody landed on my back. Then two other fellows began to rearrange my features. It was fairly dark and the guys were wearing balaclavas so I can't be sure who they were. I guess they were from the school, though, because they didn't speak – probably figured I'd recognise their voices. If some people hadn't come along, I'd probably have ended up in the canal.'

'The punks!' David struck the table with his fist. 'I'll bet they wanted to nobble you for tomorrow's basketball final.

96

Johnno wanted to know why you weren't in school today but that could have been an act.'

'I reckon so.' Billy touched his cheek gingerly. 'But, on the other hand, I decided to buy some Es from him to keep him happy. Anyway, you're the Salmon. You tell me who they were.'

'I can't,' David shrugged.

'You can't but you were able to tell Mom I was going to buy drugs,' Billy accused.

'That's because I felt responsible.' David wrung his fingers. 'Johnno tried to get me to sell tablets and I refused but I told him you might be interested.'

'Don't look so guilty.' Billy attempted a smile. 'You meant well, I guess. My mom was sure mad as hell, though.' He lowered his voice. 'She's in the lounge now with her date, the college lecturer.'

'Did you hear about Aisling?' David asked.

'No.' Billy paused in the act of sipping his drink through a straw. 'Well, out with it!'

David recounted everything that had happened, including Aisling's reaction and her note.

'I suppose I shouldn't be telling you this . . . ' Billy paused. 'It was told to me in confidence by Rebecca but what the hell – you're not a blabber-mouth. It seems Aisling's parents are breaking up. She's taking it very badly. According to Rebecca, she has overdosed on tranquillisers several times.'

'But she always seemed so normal.' David was incredulous.

'I guess that's just a front,' Billy remarked. 'You can never be sure what's going on inside a person's head.

Anyway, shaving off her hair was the latest outbreak. Now, don't mention a word of this to anyone, especially her.'

'Thanks for telling me.' David felt the weight of the world on his shoulders. If only he'd known earlier.

The entry of Mrs Jones interrupted their conversation.

'Seamus is leaving,' she announced. 'Come and say hello, Billy. You too, David.'

'Not with this face.' Billy raised his hands in protest.

'Why not?' Mrs Jones brushed his objection aside. 'I want everybody to see what's going on in this town.'

She led them into the lounge, a smell of perfume wafting behind her. To David's amazement the man who turned around to greet them was Mr Robinson, the new owner of Number 11 and the landlord of Number 8. David didn't believe for a minute that he was a man to be trusted.

'Who did this?' Mr Robinson appeared outraged.

'I haven't a clue,' Billy told him. 'They were wearing balaclavas.'

'I think it's a sad day when young people like yourself are set upon on their way home from the movies.' Mr Robinson buttoned his jacket. 'If only we could have policemen back on the beat instead of driving about in their flashy patrol cars, we'd have less of this hooliganism. I'm going to complain personally to the garda superintendent.'

'Oh, would you?' Mrs Jones reached for his hand. 'He'd be sure to listen to somebody from the institute.'

'Leave it to me, Janet.' Mr Robinson patted her hand. 'And who is this young man?' He regarded David with a benign gaze.

'David Byrne, sir.' David decided to take a risk. 'I live in Meadow Park Drive.'

'Do you?' A slight shadow flickered in Mr Robinson's keen eyes, then he continued suavely, 'I suppose you're in the same class as Billy.'

'No, sir.' David felt a chill he couldn't explain. 'Billy is in Class 2F and I'm in Class 2C.'

'Mr Keane, the principal, thought it would be better for Billy to go into Second Year because of the difference between the American and Irish systems,' Mrs Jones explained. 'I've told Billy that if he has any problems with his math or science, you'll be able to help him.'

'I've probably forgotten all my second level maths.' Mr Robinson smiled ruefully. 'Nevertheless, I'm sure I could get one of my students to give Billy a grind. Now, I'd better shove off. A packet of frozen peas is one of the best things for that lip,' he remarked to Billy as he walked to the door with Mrs Jones holding his arm.

David felt trapped. Mr Robinson was obviously a phoney, yet if he told Mrs Jones, she might never forgive him. Pretending to be short taken, he headed for the toilet. Once inside he chewed his thumb. Instantly, images came swirling in, bright and clear: a battered blue Ford Fiesta pulling into the driveway of a two-storey house with three cars parked before it, one of them the Volvo; a well-dressed woman opening the front door; two pretty girls running out to greet Mr Robinson, each of them taking one of his hands; Mr Robinson smiling at the woman as they all went indoors.

Losing no time, David returned to Billy. 'What sort of car is Mr Robinson driving?' he asked.

'A blue jalopy.' Billy peered through the net curtain. 'Last time it was a grey one. They must pay lecturers peanuts.'

David looked out and saw Mr Robinson walking towards a blue Ford Fiesta parked some distance away. 'Billy,' he said, 'I want you to ask your mother to phone the institute. They're probably closed now but she should do it first thing in the morning. Get her to ask for Mr Robinson. Don't ask me why; I just have a feeling that something's not on the level.'

CHAPTER 18

Despite his injuries, Billy was waiting outside Pine Lawns next morning. He was damned if he'd allow a mugging to keep him from playing in the match against Kilbride College, especially as it was the County Final.

'Did your mother phone the institute?' David enquired.

Billy nodded. 'They said that Robinson used to work there as a maintenance engineer but was dismissed for some unspecified reason. Naturally, Mom is upset – though she did have her suspicions. She reckoned he was a tad too coy about his academic background.'

'He's also married.' David recounted his vision of the previous evening. 'I didn't want to tell you till I knew how your mam would react.'

'Mom is a tough cookie,' Billy assured him. 'You don't survive in the Big Apple without plenty of grit – Dad couldn't hack it, I guess. That's why he took to booze and drugs – or so Mom says. By the way, I ran off those Mountjoy postcards. I'll get our gang to slip them into the punks' lockers. Mom can post the ones to the heavies in Dublin.'

'What are you going to do with the tablets you bought from Johnno?' David quickened his pace to match his friend's.

'Keep them for evidence.' Billy's bruised face lit up. 'The plastic bag should have his finger prints on it. With those and my photos— Hi!' He broke off to wave to the punks, who were jeering at them from the opposite footpath.

'What happened, Coco Pops?' Johnno shouted. 'Run into a door?'

'No,' Billy informed him, 'I got jumped by three yellow-bellies who didn't have the guts to take me on, man to man.'

'What's he talking about?' Johnno remarked to his sidekicks. 'Do any of you know who he's referring to?'

The punks guffawed but left off their taunting.

Aisling came up to David while he was removing books from his locker.

'Hi there.' She grinned shyly.

'Hi.' He grinned too. 'Thanks for your note.'

'And for yours.' She hesitated, then plunged ahead. 'I thought you were slagging me at the time – that's why I was so mad.'

'No, I was just . . . just trying to be clever, I guess.' He found her eyes even more luminous than before. 'I really did think your hair was lovely – of course, it still is. You know what I mean.'

'That's all right,' she assured him. 'You're not the only one who was appalled. Mam and Dad nearly went through the roof.'

'Can I feel your hair?' He was amazed at his own daring.

'Okay!' Her tone was matter of fact.

Gingerly he lowered his open hand onto the crown of her head; an electric current seemed to jump upward into his palm. He snatched his hand away but not before one of her classmates had seen it.

'Watch out, Aisling!' she warned. 'That's the Romeo of 2C.' David blushed.

'We'd better get to our classes.' Aisling suppressed a smile. 'I'll meet you here at the break.'

During English class Timmy, the principal, announced over the intercom that since Tuesday was St Patrick's Day, there would be no school on Monday. When the cheering died down, his voice could be heard saying something about the Chill Out Disco on Sunday night.

'Are you going to the disco, sir?' a girl asked Tubby.

'Only if you take me, my dear.' Tubby gave her an arch smile. 'Now open your books at page forty-four. In view of New York's historic contribution to the St Patrick's Day phenomenon, we will study Montague's poem "The Cage".'

Tubby was always finding an excuse to study some poem or other. Not that 'The Cage' wasn't interesting. It was about Montague's father, who had worked as a token seller in a Brooklyn subway station.

'From the evidence in the poem, how well do you think the poet and his father got on?' Tubby pressed the tips of his fingers lightly together.

There was dead silence.

'Oh, come now!' Tubby took a deep breath then released it audibly through his pursed lips. 'That's not a very difficult question.'

'I think they were probably closer in Brooklyn than in Ireland.'

Emboldened by the memory of Aisling's smile, David spoke up.

'Not a bad start,' Tubby encouraged. 'And why do you think they were closer in Brooklyn?'

'The father might have been drinking because he was unhappy and the poet as a young boy might have sensed this and felt sympathetic.'

David's face was burning with self-consciousness.

'Excellent!' Tubby pronounced. 'Excellent! Any other opinion?'

'I think that if he drank he probably beat his children,' Dermo Campbell ventured.

'But where does it say that in the poem?' Tubby tried to conceal his irritation. 'Yes, Orla. What do you think?'

'I think the poet loved his father but he felt disappointed in him,' Orla Meehan declared with her usual certainty. 'When they were back in Ireland they did not share the same dream.'

David's mind drifted to the time his father had given him the panda. It was his birthday and he was already in bed when his father arrived home. Ignoring his mother's pleas not to wake the children, he lunged past her into the bedroom. 'This is for you, son,' he announced, his breath reeking of whiskey. Then he stroked David's hair.

'Another excellent comment.' Tubby beamed at Orla. 'What was the end of a journey for one was the beginning of a journey for the other. Would you agree?'

David's thoughts wandered again. This time he was in Fennor cemetery while his father's coffin was being lowered into a black, rectangular pit. His mother was holding Darren and Emma by the hand and tears were trickling down her face. Did she love his father or had his drinking turned her against him? Maybe they were too different to get on, his mother a city woman, hard working and practical, his father like Uncle Fintan, a bit of a dreamer? And now Doug was trying to take his place.

'Master Byrne!' Tubby's voice roused him. 'You're not going to retreat into your old daydreaming state, I hope? Not after today's renaissance!'

CHAPTER 19

At breaktime Aisling was waiting near the locker. 'Let's eat our lunches outside,' she suggested. 'That way we can talk in peace.'

Even though it was March, it was a dry, mild day. Daffodils and narcissi were in bloom in the flower beds and a blackbird was singing from the top of a cypress tree. Feeling that all eyes were on them, David walked with Aisling to the football pitch, which was within full view of the staff room. The punks wouldn't hassle him there.

Two teams of junior girls were playing camogie and the game was being refereed by Michelle, a PE teacher. David and Aisling were the only spectators but already other students were wandering over from the front entrance.

'Did the cops question you about the guys who tried to pull you into the car?' David opened his sandwiches.

'Yes, the two who were in the school, Noel Morrison and Sheila Gately, called to our house.' She accepted one of his sandwiches. 'They seemed to know about the attack, so I told them everything – except about you turning up. How come you were there just then?'

David decided it wasn't yet time to tell her he was the Salmon. 'I phoned your house because I wanted to talk to you,' he explained. 'Your mother said you had gone for groceries so I headed for the supermarket.'

'And what did you want to talk to me about?' She looked straight into his eyes.

'About you and Tom,' he blurted out. 'I wanted to know why you went out with him.'

'What did you expect after the way you behaved?' she cried.

'After the way I behaved?' he echoed her words. 'How did I behave?'

'We went to Dublin that Saturday and you never asked me out afterwards or even phoned me.' She spoke heatedly. 'What was I to assume?'

David was amazed. 'I thought we would meet in school,' he said lamely.

'That's all very well,' she remarked, 'but it's not special. It's just that I have to get out of our house on weekends or I'll go mad. Tom is like a big brother to me.'

A shift in the game brought the action to their vicinity, giving David time to think. How could he admit that he couldn't ask her out because his mother always wanted him home by ten? When a girl sent the sliotar down the field with a whack of her camán, he remarked casually, 'If you like we could hang out in Billy's house. His mam is sound.'

'Great!' she agreed.

'Of course we'd have to leave about half nine or so,' he inspected his sandwich thoughtfully, 'just in case we were in the way.'

'That's fine.' She took a sip from her can of Coke. 'You could walk me home afterwards.'

'Okay.' How on earth could he walk to her house and still get home by ten?

'You don't sound very enthusiastic,' she accused. 'Is there somebody else you're seeing?'

'No!' He shook his head vigorously.

'Are you sure?' she teased. 'I think there's far more to you, Dave Byrne, than meets the eye – the fearless way you came to my rescue on Wednesday.'

'That was just a spur of the moment thing.' He tried to hide his delight.

'I'm not so sure.' She smiled mischievously. 'You are going to ask me to the disco, aren't you?'

'Sure!' David hoped that by some miracle he would be able to keep his word. 'We'll talk about it later,' he added as a group of their friends came up.

'Look, Aisling! You're in the paper!' Rebecca Dolan held up the *Lisheen Leader*.

On the front page there was a big headline: CRIMEWAVE HITS LISHEEN and under it in bold type a number of subheadings: Pensioner Attacked; Estates Vandalised; Drug Menace; Abduction Attempt; Youth Assaulted and Garda Appeal.

'I don't want to see that rag!' Aisling pushed the paper away.

'Can I take a look?' David skimmed through the article till he came to the paragraph on Billy, who was referred to as 'an African American student attending the Post Primary.' He had been set upon by 'a group of vicious thugs high on ecstasy'. The final paragraph asked the Salmon to contact the gardaí. His identity would be kept secret and there was a £500 reward from *Crime Stoppers* waiting for him.

'Why are you reading that drivel?' Aisling pouted.

'I just wanted to see what they wrote about Billy.' David handed the paper back to Rebecca.

'Is he playing against Kilbride?' Sinéad Foley asked.

'Yeah,' David said. 'The punks couldn't stop him.'

During woodwork class David thought about the article as he planed a piece of timber for a magazine rack. How could he get his hands on that £500 without letting the police know who he was? Maybe Billy would have some ideas. He adjusted the timber in the vice. The reporter had suggested that a city drug baron was extending his operations to Lisheen. Could Mr Robinson, the man who had deceived Mrs Jones, be Mr Big? He was a landlord who could use his old cars to deliver drugs without arousing suspicion.

Pretending he had hurt his thumb, David chewed it. A car parked in a lay-by bright with gorse bushes floated into his mind. The biker was removing a package from the boot. He then closed the boot, put the package in the side-carrier of his motorbike and sped away. The parked car was a blue Fiesta. Bingo!

But if Mr Robinson was a drug baron, why had Doug been talking to him? Could it be that Doug was bringing in drugs from the continent in his truck? David would have to ask Billy if Mr Robinson had let anything slip in his mother's hearing that might give a clue to his drugs operation.

'Sorry for interrupting your classes.' Timmy's voice crackled from the intercom. He announced that the basketball team had won an upset victory over Kilbride and that the star of the match had been Second Year student Billy Jones. The woodwork room erupted in raucous jubilation, a few of the messers even jumping up on work benches.

'Down!' John Joe, the teacher, roared. 'Down or you'll all be writing a hundred lines!'

He winked at David to show he wasn't really cross.

Grinning to himself, David resumed his planing. Billy's victory, coming on top of the article in the *Leader*, would rile the punks. The storm clouds were gathering.

CHAPTER 20

'Stop pushing!' Darren told Emma.

'You stop!' Emma retorted.

It was Saturday morning and David, Darren and Emma were sitting in the back seat of Doug's Audi, which was speeding towards the city.

'If you two don't stop squabbling, there won't be any burgers and chips,' Mrs Byrne threatened from the passenger seat. 'We haven't gone a mile and already you're at it. Why can't you be quiet like your big brother?'

David said nothing. He had only agreed to go on this 'family outing', as Doug called it, on the condition that he would be allowed to attend the disco. Now he was paying the price! Instead of meeting Aisling in Billy's as they had planned, he was going to be dragged round the zoo. Did Doug think he was a kid who had nothing better to do than gawk at animals in cages?

There were other things preying on his mind as well. He had phoned the police with information about Mr Robinson's car sitting in the lay-by with a package in its boot but chances were they wouldn't locate the Fiesta or arrest the biker. They always seemed to arrive too late. Meanwhile, Mr Robinson could have told Doug about meeting David in Billy's house. Suppose Billy had let slip to his mother that David was the Salmon and she had accidentally told Mr Robinson? That would mean that Doug knew too.

Anxiously chewing his thumb, he saw Doug and a man in a raincoat talking by the hippo pool. The man looked tough and efficient. Was he one of Mr Robinson's henchmen? And only this morning his mother had been telling Doug how she had found out from Garda Morrison that Mr Robinson lived in Kilbride. If Doug decided that his mother was a threat, they could all be in danger.

David looked at the close-cropped ginger hair visible above the head rest. Doug never said much when he was driving, preferring to listen to Elvis Presley tapes. Right now 'Love me Tender' was playing and his mother was smiling at Doug. It was sickening.

He chewed his thumb again, hoping to find out more about Doug, but instead, a cemetery rose before his mind's eye, headstones looming eerily in the half-light. A mixed group of teenagers, including the punks, Nick and Dermo Campbell and Lisa Cox, were standing on the graves, smoking, popping pills and drinking. Johnno put his shoulder against a headstone; Mack and Muller joined him and together they rocked and pushed. When the headstone toppled the watchers jumped up and down with excitement.

David wanted to learn more but the vision dissolved and he was back in the car. Suppose the headstone was his father's? There were two cemeteries, Fennor and St

Mary's, and he couldn't be sure which one he had seen in the vision or when it would happen.

'Was Johnno's crowd near our house recently?' he asked Emma.

'Yes.' She looked up from her pop magazine. 'They were trying to catch Tiger last night. I saw them from my bedroom. Tiger scratched and bit Johnno's hands. You should have heard him cursing!'

'Why didn't you tell me?' Mrs Byrne turned round.

'I was going to this morning,' Emma explained, 'but you told me not to bother you.'

'Sorry,' Mrs Byrne grinned apologetically.

Even without Doug's presence to complicate things, the visit to the zoo would have been disappointing. Many of the animals such as the tigers and black bears that David had enjoyed watching with his father were gone and some of the monkey houses were empty.

When they were walking downhill to the sea lions, Doug whispered something to Mrs Byrne and doubled back. Pretending that he had to go to the toilet, David followed him and, sure enough, the man in the raincoat was standing by the hippo pool, smoking a cigarette. Doug approached him, they shook hands and soon they were engaged in an intense conversation. There was no way that David could get close enough to hear anything so after a few minutes he turned back.

Doug caught up with them by the orang-utan house. 'These used to be my favourites.' He indicated a sad looking orang-utan contemplating them from his concrete prison while another smaller one picked up a peanut David had thrown to him.

'You're not supposed to feed the animals,' Mrs Byrne remarked mildly. 'They get a balanced diet.'

'It won't do him any harm.' David threw another peanut.

'You should do what your mother tells you, David,' Doug remonstrated.

'I want to go home.' David walked off.

Doug followed him. 'David, you and I will have to have a talk.' He laid his hand on David's shoulder.

David shook it off.

'Look,' Doug's voice hardened, 'I'm doing my best to be reasonable. Your mother works like a slave in that café to keep you all fed and clothed. Couldn't you give her one nice day to remember?'

'I didn't want to come!' David saw a group of Americans with emerald green ties and scarves gazing at him and realised that they thought he was behaving like a spoilt brat.

'You'll find that when you're my age you often have to do things you don't feel like doing,' Doug told him quietly.

David glanced at him, puzzled. Was Doug being sincere or was he just putting on an act?

'There's one other thing, which I wasn't going to bring up till later.' Doug took a small brown envelope from his coat pocket. 'Your mother came across the pawn ticket in your wardrobe and we decided to redeem it – no questions asked. Go on, open it. It's your Omega.'

Next day in church, Father Moore spoke about the vandalism that had taken place overnight in St Mary's Cemetery – David thanked God that it wasn't Fennor. Father Moore said that it was difficult to comprehend what drove young people to carry out such acts. David had phoned the police as soon as he had returned from the zoo and left a message for Garda Morrison, naming the vandals. He wondered if his message had been passed on. The operator had been quite friendly – he suspected that she wanted to keep him on the line so that the police could trace the call.

'In my experience,' Father Moore's voice broke in on his thoughts, 'many vandals come from middle-class homes. Maybe they are deprived, not of material possessions, but of love and spiritual values.'

David scrutinised the seats before him, hoping to catch a glimpse of Aisling's exquisite head. When he phoned her house the previous evening her mother had said she was out with friends. Did that mean she had gone back to Tom? The Chill Out Disco was being held in the parish hall that night. He would have talk to her and make sure they were going together.

CHAPTER 21

David, dressed in combats and a dark shirt, was dancing with the Kelts, hoping nobody noticed his lack of rhythm. Beside him Aisling in a grey skirt, red top and knee-high 'Hooker' boots was moving gracefully in time to the Oasis beat, her face lit up with excitement. Rebecca was twisting near Billy and Sinéad was bobbing between Maurice and Tom so that between them they formed a shifting circle.

There was a great atmosphere in the hall: all around them coloured lights flashed in sync with the amplified music, bodies jerked and tossed like puppets and a mixed odour of perfume, cigarette smoke and perspiration filled the air.

Despite his pleasure in being with Aisling, David felt uneasy. Johnno and his sidekicks were watching him from the vicinity of the door and when he had tried to go to the toilet they had moved to follow. He could guess why they were sore. Tom had told him that Lisa Cox and Dermo Campbell were nabbed by the cops the previous night as they fled from the graveyard and this evening Billy had seen Noel Morrison and Sheila Gately frisking the punks in Main Street while the patrol car waited nearby. It was unlikely the punks would touch him in the hall but on the way home, after the disco he would almost certainly be jumped. Even the 'equaliser' that Billy had given him, a vial of Mace belonging to his mother, mightn't be of much use. Nevertheless, he felt his pocket to make sure he still had it.

As Oasis faded the DJ put on U2 and the girls decided to go to the ladies. David sat near the stage, chewing his thumb anxiously. At once he had a vision of the skinhead, Nick Campbell, and another heavy sitting in a Toyota in the car park. It was the same Toyota he and Billy had seen outside 34 Manor Drive. He was now trapped.

As if to emphasise this, back in reality Johnno and his sidekicks, fags dangling from their lips, made their way to his vicinity. Then in passing, Johnno hissed, 'Goodnight, Davina.'

Use your head, David told himself. Tell one of the supervisors what's going on. No, he decided, that wouldn't work. The punks would claim they were only there for the dancing. He needed more information.

Chewing his thumb again, he saw Rebecca and Sinéad beside a washbasin, popping something into their mouths. Then they drank from the cold tap. All this time Aisling was chatting to a group of girls who were putting on make-up. The scene shifted and then Rebecca was lying on the dance floor, with Billy cradling her head.

Crikey! He would have to phone for an ambulance. There was a coin box in the foyer – but how would he get past Johnno and his sidekicks? Maybe if he got Aisling to phone? No. Who would send out an ambulance for an emergency that hadn't occurred?

Scribbling a note on the inside of an empty cigarette box he rose and drifted over to Mrs Keogh, a supervisor who looked friendly. When he was sure nobody was watching, he asked her to give the note to the DJ.

'And now for all you Michael Jackson fans, it's "History"!' the DJ was announcing as David wormed his way back through the jostling throng. When he reached the Kelts, Aisling put her hands on his shoulders, and with a mixture of nervousness and joy he rested his fingers on her waist. Rebecca and Sinéad began dancing with wild abandon, seemingly possessed of Wacko Jacko's feverish energy. David moved closer to Aisling and speaking into her ear to make himself heard above the music, asked who was selling Es.

'Campbell's sister, Jackie, and Lisa Cox were selling them in the bog.' She put her mouth close to his ear so that he could feel her breath. 'Some of the girls bought them. Why do you ask?'

'Oh, just curious.' He kissed her ear.

'I haven't taken any, if that's what you're afraid of.' She smiled archly.

On and on the music blared, the pace fast and furious. While he was hopping in front of Aisling a question kept gnawing at David's brain: would the DJ dismiss his note as a hoax? Already he had put on the Spice Girls' 'If you wannabe my lover' and the din and flashing lights were beginning to give David a headache. The other Kelts, however, moved into higher gear, jumping and shouting to the words. Even Aisling seemed to be caught up in the frenzy.

Finally the music came to an end and the DJ called for attention. Would John Cox, Iggy MacDermott and Jim

Mullooly go to the car park, where their presence was urgently required?

'It's the cops, lads!' somebody shouted, causing an outburst of laughter as the trio moved through the crowd.

The music started again. Excusing himself, David hurried out to the foyer. Quickly he dialled 999 and putting on a deep voice, asked for an ambulance, giving his name as John Duignan, the vice principal. Pressing down the hook, he dialled 999 again and left a message for Garda Morrison concerning Campbell and the heavies in the Toyota. When the operator asked for his name he told her he was the Salmon.

On impulse he decided to phone his mother.

'Could Doug pick me up in the car park at eleven thirty?' he asked 'It's urgent!'

Before he could give an explanation, he heard the punks being questioned by the doorman. Hanging up the receiver, he slipped into the hall just as the entrance door opened. With any luck he hadn't been spotted.

'You're looking worried,' Aisling shouted. 'Is anything wrong?'

Trying to ignore the punks, who had stopped only a few feet away, David shook his head. 'I just want to tell Billy something,' he mouthed.

Before he could speak to his friend, however, Billy and Rebecca moved off with Maurice and Sinéad towards the mineral bar. Unwilling to leave Aisling on her own with Tom, David didn't follow. Instead he invited her to go with him for a Coke.

'Can't we go later?' she demurred.

Caught between Tom and the punks, he decided that he had to continue dancing. Luckily, the DJ put on Boyzone's slow number 'Words'. Aisling threw her arms around his neck and with her cheek resting on his shoulder they moved together under the gaze of the punks. This was the moment David had dreamt about, yet he was on a knife edge. Would the ambulance and police arrive in time? Then a daring idea occurred to him.

'Come on,' he said to Aisling. 'I want to talk to Johnno.'

CHAPTER 22

As David approached, Johnno stared at him in disbelief.

'Have you any E-tablets left?' David spoke in a voice loud enough to be heard over the music. 'I'm knackered.'

'Get lost, Byrne!' Mack snapped. 'Do you want to get us thrown out?'

'No,' David shook his head.

'Why did you have us called out to the car park?' Johnno grabbed his arm.

'What are you on about?' David pretended to be surprised. 'I never went near the DJ. Why? What happened?'

'Never you mind what happened.' Johnno sounded less sure of his ground. 'I got your postcard on Friday,' he continued, changing tack.

'I didn't send you a postcard,' David declared.

'Oh, you didn't?' Johnno tightened his grip till his fingers were digging into David's biceps. 'You and me are going to have a talk, Byrne.'

'Fine.' David betrayed no unease. 'But not till later.'

He twisted out of Johnno's hold and walked off with Aisling, knowing that the punks would not risk creating a scene.

'That was really cool!' Aisling said, pressing her mouth to his ear.

David didn't answer. He had sown doubt in Johnno's mind, but not convinced him of his innocence. Even so hopefully the punks would bide their time.

The others had returned from the mineral bar and again the circle was formed but this time the dancing was wilder, more abandoned. David tried to keep up, despite the growing dizziness that threatened to overcome him. Through a blur of pulsing light he saw Billy trying to support Rebecca, who was slumping to the ground. Beside him Aisling seemed unreal, a wind-tossed flame, shimmering and shifting. If he didn't get fresh air he would collapse.

'I have to leave,' he called out to her. 'It's an emergency.'

Before she could question him, he slipped away. The music stopped and there was a babble of anxious voices. With his heart in his mouth, he ventured out the front door. The night air hit him like an arctic blast, clearing his head.

'You're off early,' a parent who was acting as doorman remarked.

'No,' David told him. 'I just came out for some air.'

There was nobody visible at the exit gates or at the sides of the building. A few cars were parked beyond the arc of light at the front entrance. Which of them was the Toyota?

Deciding that the doorman would raise the alarm if he were attacked, he ventured within a dozen feet of the parked cars. They probably belonged to the organisers of the disco. There were seven cars in all – but no sign of the

Toyota. Had Nick and the heavies decided to wait down the road? He chewed his thumb but nothing came. Uncertain, he returned to the doorman.

'Did you see a Toyota parked here?' he asked.

'I sure did.' The doorman flicked away the cigarette end he was smoking. 'A patrol car pulled in about fifteen minutes ago and it took off like a bat out of hell. For all I know, the patrol car is still chasing— What's that?' he exclaimed, hurrying indoors as a commotion broke out.

David was on the point of following when out barged Johnno and his sidekicks. David fled.

The punks were in no hurry as they followed him. They would wait till they were out of sight of the hall before closing in for the kill. David's only chance was to reach Main Street, which was well lit.

Fear spurring him on, he hared out the entrance and down the road towards the town. He was tired, however, and the punks gained on him relentlessly. With lungs bursting he tried to put on a fresh spurt. It was useless. Outside the parish church he turned, waving the Mace to keep them at bay.

'Stay back or I'll use this,' he gasped. The punks halted.

'What is it?' Johnno panted. 'Your perfume spray?'

'No,' David swung the container menacingly. 'It's Mace.'

'Mace.' Johnno pretended to double up with laughter. 'Sure only women use that.'

'What a wuss!' Mack sneered.

'Here, Davina, hand it over.' Johnno stretched out his open palm.

'I'm warning you!' David backed against the wall as the punks closed in.

'And I'm warning you.' Shielding his eyes with his left hand, Johnno grabbed blindly with his right.

Quick as lightning David kicked him in the shin then sprayed Mack and Muller in the eyes before they could cover them. Their howls made Johnno retreat. David followed him, his whole being possessed with fury.

'Who's the woman now?' he demanded.

For answer Johnno sprang at him with eyes closed but some of the Mace hit him before his momentum sent David toppling backward. The two of them rolled over on the ground, Johnno cursing and flailing wildly with his fists, David punching and clawing with every ounce of strength he possessed. He knew it was only a matter of seconds until he was smashed into unconsciousness but before that happened he meant to leave his mark on his adversary. One of his fists must have connected with Johnno's chin because suddenly he wasn't being pummelled any longer. Then he became aware of Tom Farrell's voice and saw him dragging the inert Johnno over to the footpath, where the other two punks were being held down by Maurice.

'Are you all right, cara?' Tom returned and helped David to his feet.

'I'm fine,' David brushed the hair out of his eyes.

'That was a brilliant scrap,' Tom said admiringly. 'I didn't think you had it in you.'

To hide his confusion, David asked, 'How's Rebecca?'

'Not good,' Tom said. 'An ambulance arrived really quickly, though. Aisling sent us after you when she noticed that the punks had left the hall.'

CHAPTER 23

David had just located the Mace container in bushes near the roadside when Doug's Audi screeched to a halt.

'Why are you waiting here?' Doug called out as he rolled down the window. 'And what on earth happened to you?'

An exhausted David explained all that had occurred, with Tom adding that Noel Morrison and Sheila Gately had just driven off with the punks.

'Bloody gits! I'll pulverise them,' Doug declared. 'Tiger's gone missing too – I wonder if they have anything to do with that. But come on, hop in.'

'Can we give Aisling a lift?' David eased himself into the passenger seat, his muscles aching. 'She's still at the disco.'

Back at the hall they found that Aisling had gone with Rebecca in the ambulance, the paramedic having refused to let Billy accompany her. Tom and Maurice were staying with Sinéad but Billy decided to take a lift in the Audi.

On the way home Doug discussed Rebecca's collapse with Billy while David sat chewing his thumb. He felt certain that the punks were responsible for Tiger's disappearance. Almost instantly a vision of Tiger peeping out through the slats of an orange crate entered his mind. The crate was sitting on the floor of what looked like a prefab because the walls were made of wood which had been sprayed with graffiti and a naked bulb hung from the plasterboard ceiling. There was a disused prefab near the Harbour Field that the owner used to rent to students. It was worth a try.

'Can we drive to Kilroy's prefab?' David interrupted. 'I've a feeling that the punks may have hidden Tiger there.'

'Fair enough,' Doug agreed. 'I'll give Joan a buzz.'

He took out his mobile phone with his left hand, pressed some buttons and while steering with his right hand explained to David's mother that they would be delayed.

'You go to bed, Joan,' he concluded. 'I can let myself and David in.'

The prefab was enclosed on three sides by a whitethorn hedge so that it was partially screened from view. The walls and roof were weather beaten and black plastic bags covered the windows.

'Do you know that if you're caught in there you could be up for breaking and entering?' Doug observed.

'We'll take our chances.' David wondered if Doug was concerned for their safety or for what they might find inside.

He and Billy pushed open the rusty iron gate and tiptoed down the gravel path, leaving Doug to park the car where he could keep a look-out for anybody approaching.

The door of the prefab was closed. In the light from a distant street lamp Billy forced the lock with his plastic phone card.

As they stepped inside a rank smell assailed their nostrils. When Billy had closed the door David flicked on the switch, flooding the interior with harsh light. The sight that met their eyes was disgusting. Cigarette butts and empty beer cans littered the floor, garbage was heaped in the corners and weird graffiti adorned the walls, to which car registration plates had been nailed in random fashion. Bunk beds with dirty blankets, one on either side of the room, looked as if they had recently been used, while a small electric heater stood near the back wall.

A plaintive miaow drew David's attention to the orange crate which had been placed behind a chair. Quickly he removed the concrete block weighing the crate down and raised one edge, whereupon Tiger shot out and disappeared under the nearest bed. David knelt down to pull him out but Tiger hissed at him.

'Look here!' Billy indicated a chalk drawing of a cat with a block tied to its neck. Above it there was a salmon with knives and spears sticking out of wounds from which blood dripped on to a printed caption: YOU DIE TONIGHT. Various slogans, some racial, others about drugs, were scrawled beside the picture.

'Those punks are right sickos.' David felt angry for his friend.

'I'd say they were stoned out of their minds,' Billy observed. 'The dumb jerks have even signed their initials. Look at—!'

He broke off as the soft crunching of gravel reached them. Turning off the light, David partly opened the door and peeped out. In the uncertain light he could see Doug approaching.

'Hurry!' Doug called out softly. 'Someone's coming.'

'I'm just going to get Tiger.' David let Billy out, closed the door after him and switched on the light. Using a greasy paper bag that smelled of fish and chips he coaxed Tiger out from under the bed then grabbed him before he could run off.

With Tiger clutched to his chest, he switched off the light, pulled the door closed and joined Billy and Doug, who were waiting impatiently. They hurried across to the whitethorn hedge and with not a moment to spare found a gap through which they squeezed. Unaware that he was being watched, a fellow walked up to the prefab, cast a furtive glance behind him, then opened the door with a key. It was Nick Campbell!

'Gotcha!' Doug whispered. He took out his mobile phone. 'You fellows wait in the car,' he instructed. 'I left it unlocked.'

Keeping a firm hold on Tiger, David tiptoed off with Billy. Was Doug phoning the police or Mr Robinson? Getting rid of himself and Billy didn't make sense.

'I wonder how Rebecca's doing,' Billy said when they were seated in the car. 'I warned her about pills but she's stubborner than hell.'

'She'll be fine once she's in hospital.' David tried to reassure him. 'Weren't we lucky that Campbell didn't find us in the prefab?'

They waited for what seemed an eternity, David's suspicions about Doug growing by the minute. Though he chewed his thumb no vision came. Then as he was about to suggest to Billy that they should leave, a patrol car came speeding by. It halted before reaching the metal gate and turned off its lights. Two gardaí emerged and headed towards the prefab. So Doug had been on the level all along! David winced at his own stupidity.

After another interminable wait, Doug came striding up. 'Well, David, that was a lucky hunch of yours,' he declared, starting the engine. 'The guards found a stash of E-tablets in the prefab and Campbell had more on his person.'

'Did they catch the other guys who were with him in the Toyota, the skinhead and his mate?' David asked.

'I think so,' Doug put the engine in gear. 'The guards wouldn't say much but Campbell must have legged it and taken the train back to Lisheen. He probably intended to spend the night in the prefab.'

Doug eased the car slowly off the grass margin on to the road. 'Keep a tight hold on that cat,' he warned over his shoulder. 'I don't want him jumping about while I'm driving.'

David barely heard him. He was recalling the vision that he had had during woodwork class of the biker taking a package from Mr Robinson's Fiesta. Now that most of the heavies had been arrested would the drop still go ahead?

CHAPTER 24

'You're sure this is the right place?' Doug lowered his binoculars and looked at David, who was examining a new telephoto camera. They were lying on a raincoat behind a low bank which hid them from the view of anybody travelling the Kilbride Road, two hundred yards below. Noel Morrison and Sheila Gately had dropped them off at 12.45 pm and it was now 1.55.

'Unless there's another lay-by with gorse bushes,' David replied. Even at this distance the yellow blossoms were visible in the watery sunlight.

'According to Noel this is the only one within a radius of forty miles,' Doug conceded. 'I'll give him another buzz.' He picked up his mobile phone and pressed a button.

'Hi, Noel,' he drawled. 'Any activity at your end?' After listening for a few seconds, he added, 'We'll give him another half hour', and put down the phone. 'If only we could be sure he hasn't made the drop already . . .' He scratched the stubble on his chin. 'The fact that the guards arrested Campbell and that skinhead and his mate last night may have scared our Mr Robinson off. Are you positive Mrs Jones said Monday?'

'Yes,' David assured him. 'She told Billy she heard him talking on the phone to somebody while they were driving back from Dublin. "The goods will be in the lay-by, the one with the gorse bushes, on Monday at 1.45 pm," he said.'

Even as he spoke David was aware that he wasn't telling the whole truth since Billy's mother hadn't heard any reference to gorse bushes. He had persuaded Doug to let him accompany him on the stakeout in return for the information. Though at first Doug had objected, citing David's bruises and the danger, he had finally relented. David figured Doug was really an undercover cop and the binoculars and telephoto camera seemed to confirm it.

'How can you be sure Mr Robinson is Mr Big?' he decided to probe a little further.

'Can you keep a secret?' Doug fixed him with his keen glance. David nodded. 'It was me who first put the guards on to Robinson.' Doug lowered his voice as if he feared the cattle grazing nearby might overhear him. 'He offered me a lot of money – thousands, in fact – to carry parcels from the continent in my truck, so I tipped off the drugs unit. They've had Robinson under surveillance for months but he's a slippery customer. That man you saw me talking to in the zoo was a detective – your mother told me you were quizzing her about him.'

'I'm sorry for not trusting you,' David apologised. He was about to confide in Doug that he was the Salmon but at that moment he saw him tense as he looked through the binoculars. He had sighted something.

Picking up the telephone, Doug jabbed the button and said in an urgent voice, 'The fox is coming.' Then he grabbed the telephoto camera and rose to his knees. 'Wait here,' he instructed. 'I'm going to try for a close-up. Keep an eye on me with the binoculars. If – and only if – you see anything amiss, phone Noel Morrison. You have only to press this button and speak. And whatever you do, stay out of danger or your mother will kill me.'

Before David could question him, he slipped downhill, keeping to the cover of a dry-stone wall. Quivering with excitement, David picked up the binoculars. Looking through them, he saw the blue Fiesta coming to a halt in the lay-by.

The driver got out, locked the door, then entered a lane that wound up the hill. After walking for a short while he climbed over a wall into an adjacent field. Anyone passing would probably take him for a farmer checking on his cattle, but from his build and well-cut suit, David had no doubt it was Mr Robinson. A chill ran up his spine. Would Mr Robinson spot Doug, who was now crouched behind a drinking trough? If only Billy were here to help.

David picked up the phone to speak to Noel Morrison, then put it down again. If Doug was an undercover cop he wouldn't welcome unnecessary panic.

Mr Robinson was still coming uphill, walking casually as if he had nothing to hide. When he reached a clump of blackthorns he ducked behind them, took out a small pair of binoculars and scanned the road below. David could see Doug snapping away from the cover of a gorse bush before working his way closer to his quarry. The seconds ground to a halt, heavy with menace.

To ease the tension, David chewed his thumb. With

blood-chilling clarity he saw Mr Robinson pointing a revolver at Doug, who was handing over the camera. The soft thunder of a motorbike brought him back to the present. Doug had vanished and through the binoculars he could see the biker entering the lay-by. There wasn't a moment to lose.

Pressing the button on the mobile, he informed Noel about everything that was taking place, then pocketing the phone and leaving the binoculars on the overcoat, he headed downhill, bent low, heart pounding. Venturing through a gap in a stone wall, he saw Mr Robinson's back and, facing him, Doug. Nerves stretched to breaking point, he picked his way to within a dozen feet of them before a loud ringing betrayed his presence. The bloody phone! As Mr Robinson began to turn, David charged. He was aware of Doug shouting, Mr Robinson's gun hand swinging towards his face, a jarring blow that sent pain coursing through his head, then he was sinking down into blackness.

The first thing he became aware of when he regained consciousness was a flashing blue light. He was lying on the grass and somebody was bending over him, talking gently. It was Doug. After a while he could make out the words, 'Can you hear me, David?'

'Yes,' he mumbled.

'Take it easy,' Doug said as he tried to rise. 'You got a bad bash on the head. Just stay quiet till the ambulance arrives. The guards are calling for one on their radio this minute.'

'Did they get Mr Robinson?' David winced with pain.

'They didn't have to,' Doug declared. 'I flattened him with the camera. Right now Noel and Sheila have him in the patrol car over there – they drove up the lane and into the field.'

'And the biker?' David spoke slowly.

'He didn't get far,' Doug assured him. 'The drug squad found a parcel with thousands of ecstasy tablets in his side-carrier. They're also raiding all Robinson's houses, so his drug ring is smashed. Which reminds me, you could have got us both killed by charging down like that.'

'I'm sorry,' David apologised.

'Ah, forget it,' Doug grinned. 'It was crazy but it took guts. You're quite a man, David.'

EPILOGUE

Lisheen prided itself on its St Patrick's Day parades and since the weather was dry, the number of floats was up and Compu-Tel had brought a High School band over from New York to complement the local brass-and-reed band, this year's parade promised to be the best ever.

Near the centre of the colourful line of trailers, floats and marching groups, that stretched from Meadow Park across the Canal Bridge and down to the square, David and Aisling shared a trailer with the Post Primary School's basketball team. On the float behind them St Patrick was driving the serpents out of Ireland with his crosier. Some of the serpents were offering sweets to children watching from the footpaths.

The basketball trailer had a banner reading 'COUNTY CHAMPIONS' stretched overhead. Underneath the banner, players in shorts and jerseys were tossing a ball from one to another, with Billy completing the movement by dropping it into a basket; Aisling in the role of Victory, adorned with papier-mâché wings and gold coronet, would then place a laurel wreath on his head, while David, togged out as referee, blew a whistle. Since Billy's face was still bruised and David's head was surrounded by a bandage, the spectators laughed heartily at the implied violence. The impression of mayhem was reinforced by having Sinéad as an umpire belabour offending players with a loofah.

The first time that Aisling placed the wreath on his head, Billy grinned at David and whispered, 'I wonder what my old teacher, Mike Gilmartin, would think if he saw me now?'

'He'd be envious as hell,' David assured him. 'Do you think he's getting ready to march up Fifth Avenue?'

'Not for another five hours.' Billy handed the wreath back to Aisling. 'I wish you were here, Mike.'

The only member of the Kelts not on the trailer was Rebecca, who was recovering in hospital from her near-fatal collapse. David's head injuries were not serious enough to warrant an overnight stay, though he had been advised by the intern who treated him to take it easy lest too much activity bring on delayed concussion. Nevertheless, he had argued with his mother and Doug that joining the basketball contingent would not be a risk.

While they were still discussing the matter he had let slip that he was the Salmon. At first his mother was convinced that the blow to his head was causing him to suffer delusions but when he recounted everything that had happened, including his vision of her after tasting the salmon, she had changed her mind.

'Your father's family were always a bit strange,' she reflected. 'I don't mean 'strange' in the sense of 'mad' but 'psychic'. Sure your Uncle Fintan is always going on about 'inner sightings' and 'visions'.'

Doug was much less surprised, having heard from Noel

Morrison that David was high on their list of candidates for the Salmon – it seems the gardaí had established that many of the Salmon's phone calls came from the kiosk on the edge of Meadow Park Estate. Doug also reminded them that *Crime Stoppers* had offered £500 for information leading to the smashing of the drug ring and he would be able to collect this for the Salmon without his identity being made public. The punks would very likely do six months in a reformatory, as, not only had they been in possession of ecstasy tablets when Noel and Sheila had searched them outside the church on Sunday night, but their finger prints had been found in Mrs O'Neill's house.

The news of the reward had not been the only triumph for David. He had persuaded his mother to invite Billy and Mrs Jones, as well as Aisling, to dinner that evening. He and his mother had laid out the dining room in preparation and all was now set for a fabulous get-together, after which they would visit Rebecca.

When they neared the reviewing stand at the end of Main Street, David spotted his mother and Doug among the throng of spectators. They were talking to Mrs Jones, who had on a bright green dress. Darren and Emma were not with them because they were marching with the swimming club. No sooner did Mrs Jones catch sight of the basketball contingent than she began clapping and cheering. Then his mother and Doug joined in, setting off a general outburst of applause that spread to the reviewing stand, where Timmy Keane, the principal, rose to his feet shouting, 'Well done, lads!'

David smiled at Aisling and she winked conspiratorially. This was going to be a St Patrick's Day he would remember for as long as he lived.

What the critics say about
The Stranger and the Pooka

"Patrick Devaney writes beautifully about nature, and the book has clever black and white illustrations by Don Conroy . . . "

Irish Times

"The book combines both emotional and natural beauty to form a story of mystery and intrigue."

Parent & Teacher

"I wasn't going to read this book . . . I'm very glad I did. Every now and then a children's book comes along so original in its presentation, and so thought-provoking in the issues it raises, that one can overlook its PC approach to green issues . . . "

Books Ireland

"The superbly-crafted story confronts many controversial issues, including the breakdown of the mother-and-child relationship, the difficulty of dealing with a troubled past, the effects of dark secrets revealed in a close-knit rural community and the impact of unscrupulous business dealings on the rural environment and wildlife."

Roscommon Herald